"Don't you want to tell me how I did on the dance floor tonight?" Liz asked.

"You were okay for a beginner," Joe said lightly.

"I was a hit," she insisted. "Did you see the guy with the pinkie ring—he never took his eyes off me."

"Baloney. He was watching the redhead, not you." Joe had seen the man and wanted to punch his lights out all evening.

"I don't want to go to bed yet," Liz announced, feeling momentarily brave.

"What do you want?" Joe asked, tempted to pull the zipper on her dress down.

His mouth was inches from her. It was more than she could resist. She leaned against him.

Her voice was husky as she nuzzled his ear. "I'd like you to kiss me goodnight, Joe. Out here in the hall like kids do on Saturday-night dates. If anyone catches us it'll make it all the better—I never did that when I was growing up. Being a policeman's daughter was very restricting."

He saw in her tiger eyes the passion waiting to erupt, and he knew it echoed his own.

"Kiss me, Joe. Not the way you do on the set. Kiss me like you would if we were high school sweethearts. . . ."

WHAT ARE *LOVESWEPT* ROMANCES?

They are stories of true romance and touching emotion. We believe those two very important ingredients are constants in our highly sensual and very believable stories in the *LOVESWEPT* line. Our goal is to give you, the reader, stories of consistently high quality that may sometimes make you laugh, sometimes make you cry, but are always fresh and creative and contain many delightful surprises within their pages.

Most romance fans read an enormous number of books. Those they truly love, they keep. Others may be traded with friends and soon forgotten. We hope that each *LOVESWEPT* romance will be a treasure—a "keeper." We will always try to publish

LOVE STORIES YOU'LL NEVER FORGET
BY AUTHORS YOU'LL ALWAYS REMEMBER

The Editors

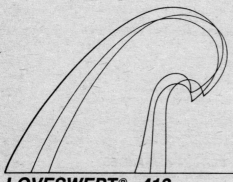

LOVESWEPT® • 412

Doris Parmett
Off Limits

 BANTAM BOOKS
NEW YORK • TORONTO • LONDON • SYDNEY • AUCKLAND

OFF LIMITS

A Bantam Book / July 1990

LOVESWEPT® and the wave device are registered
trademarks of Bantam Books, a division of
Bantam Doubleday Dell Publishing Group, Inc.
Registered in U.S. Patent
and Trademark Office and elsewhere.

If you would be interested in receiving protective vinyl
covers for your Loveswept books, please write to this address
for information:

Loveswept
Bantam Books
P.O. Box 985
Hicksville, NY 11802

ISBN 0-553-44042-X

Published simultaneously in the United States and Canada

Bantam Books are published by Bantam Books, a division
of Bantam Doubleday Dell Publishing Group, Inc. Its trademark, consisting of the words "Bantam Books" and the
portrayal of a rooster, is Registered in U.S. Patent and
Trademark Office and in other countries. Marca Registrada.
Bantam Books, 666 Fifth Avenue, New York, New York
10103.

PRINTED IN THE UNITED STATES OF AMERICA

OPM   0 9 8 7 6 5 4 3 2 1

One

Liz Davis licked her ruby-red lips and raised her long slender arms, reaching for the man whose deep blue eyes reminded her of smooth, unruffled velvet. Those eyes were now blazing with the heat of passion. His fingers slowly ran down her naked thigh, lingering at the back of her knee, drawing circles in the hollows of her sensitive flesh, making her gasp with pleasure.

Alert to her every nuance, he watched her magnificent face until he felt her long red nails dig into his flesh. It was their signal. Only the faint rustle of limbs adjusting to limbs against the satin sheets and the heavy sexual tempo of Ravel's *Bolero* broke the silence.

"Now, my darling. Now."

A fleeting look of power crossed the man's face as he poised above her. "Tell me again. Tell me how much you want me," he demanded in a low, throbbing baritone.

"No."

"Say it. Say it or I'll leave."

She dragged his face to hers, and almost snarled into his mouth. "I want you. Damn your soul to hell, I want you."

Having won their latest battle, he crushed her to him, giving her what they both wanted. . . .

"Cut and print," the director ordered. "That was good, kids. Lunch break, everyone." Then director Stan Bernard walked off the set with the producer and one of the writers responsible for making *Happy Town* a weekly nighttime hit soap opera.

Liz pushed her partner unceremoniously off her. Although not visible to the camera, the body stocking she wore kept her from being naked. "Joe, hasn't anyone ever told you you're supposed to *pretend* in a love scene, not really go at it?!"

Joe Michaels hopped off the bed, grinning. He was glad. It seemed he'd finally gotten the ice princess's goat, after months of her getting his. "I'm a method actor, Lizzy, my girl," he said. "My method is to enjoy myself whenever I can."

Liz threw back a wayward strand of blond hair and glared at his six-foot frame. She knew women all over the country envied her. His fan mail bulged like his biceps. The girls in the office would drool as he sauntered by, giving a special hello for each. No doubt about it, he was a charmer. He remembered birthdays with flowers. If one of the crew was in trouble, he'd listen patiently, offering helpful advice and unasked-for donations. His handsome, rugged looks and easygoing manner attracted women of all ages, women who wanted a piece of the action. And the action was Joe Michaels. He was definitely a hunk—a hunk with brains who avidly devoured *The New York Times* and *The Wall Street Journal* while awaiting his turn on the set.

When Liz first learned she'd be getting a new male costar, she'd read Joe's bio, and hadn't believed a word of it. According to the press release he'd been born in Colorado, had come East to attend Harvard, and had been sidetracked by the lure of the stage.

"Is this true?" she'd asked her agent. "Is Joe really a Harvard graduate?"

"Scout's honor. Your estimable costar was a classmate of the producer's son. No dope, that one. He's Phi Beta Kappa."

Now she stretched her hand toward her handsome costar. She knew it was best to use the straightforward approach with him. "Truce, Joe. I'll bring lunch tomorrow. Let's see if we can stand each other in the close-ups."

He gave her a look that made her shiver from her head to her toes. She hoped he couldn't see the wheels turning in her head. Despite their barely concealed antagonism, she wanted a favor from him now. She wanted him to agree to a lucrative business proposition. This morning she'd received a call, her third actually, begging her to host a talk-radio program during the off-season. The catch was they only wanted her provided she could convince Joe to be her co-anchor. According to her agent, the public saw them as a hot duo, a sizzling team. Yet, her agent told her he nixed the idea when he was approached originally, although he hadn't said why. She had to find out his reason, then change his mind. The possibility of earning extra money was too attractive—and important—to let go without a little arm-twisting.

Watching Liz's beautiful face frown in concentration, Joe restrained an impulse to laugh. Though she was often standoffish, he could see the wheels turning in the ice princess's pretty head. He decided to humor her.

"Okay, Lizzy, tuna it is. Provided you make the sandwiches. No store-bought salad drowning in mayo."

"My treat," she agreed, wanting to swat him for calling her Lizzy. Smiling guilelessly, she made a mental note to stop at the supermarket for albacore. Too bad they didn't sell shark!

"Hello," a female voice said.

Joe waved a cheery greeting to Shirley Richards, the gossip columnist. Her column ran in over five hundred papers and in the top movie and television magazines. She had a weekly spot on *Entertainment This Week*. He knew she hadn't been expected.

When Shirley had called earlier that morning, Liz had excused herself, saying she needed to study a last-minute script change. She would do almost anything to avoid the pint-sized piranha. But Shirley was currently engrossed with one of the other stars.

Liz refused to have anything to do with Shirley ever since the columnist had almost destroyed the career of one of Liz's friends.

A prop man walked toward them, preparing to adjust a desk for the next scene. "Cal," Joe said. "My body's rebelling from the board you're palming off as a mattress. How about a water bed for a change of pace? How about it, Liz?"

"Oh, no you don't, Joseph Michaels! I get seasick if I look at a pond. What happens if I have to grab you and miss?"

"Well now," Joe drawled lazily. "I expect both of us might have a little more fun if you grab something not in the script." He laughed when she blushed. So, he thought, the public Liz and the private Liz appear to be two very different persons. He filed the information away for future use.

When he'd first joined the show, his agent had told him not to bother to ask her out, should he be so inclined. "Ms. Liz Davis's private life is strictly off limits. What you see emoting on the small screen is about all she does. If there's a man in her life she's doing a good job of hiding him."

He'd howled when he'd read her bio. Depending on the release, she claimed to be born in India of British parents (dad was with the foreign service), China (dad's an importer), Paris (*maman* met *papa* at the Sorbonne, where he taught languages), Madrid (bullfighting killed him), London (very hush-hush government work), and New York (dad retired early. She didn't say from what). The bald-faced fabrications were served in a lighthearted manner, offered with such good humor that few objected. The press loved her and helped to foster her image as one of the soaps' great witches.

Joe intended to find out the truth.

He suspected the truth was that Liz was nothing like her bio. If anything, she was a closet prude in a profession where life-styles often imitated art. He had discovered she was actually born in Philadelphia to a policeman father and dietician mother, now deceased.

But he did have to admire how well she played the siren. Liz Davis made love to the camera. The lens caressed her high cheekbones, stroked her delicate skin, adored her dainty curves, bringing out her youthful energy and sizzling passion. He wanted her. He had set about having her. Slowly.

Biding his time, he extended his contract, although his true goal was to become a producer. While he waited he was thoroughly enjoying himself, not knowing what nonsense Liz would pitch next.

He chuckled over her last interview. "Good genes and growing up near the sea. The salt air is marvelous for the skin," Liz was quoted as saying in *People* magazine when asked about her porcelain complexion. He'd teased her about that, saying the next time she told a whopper he'd let everyone know she hailed from Philadelphia. She'd replied by sticking out her tongue at him. "And spoil their fun? Shame on you, you naughty boy."

Joe stared down at her upturned face, wondering what would happen if he leaned over to kiss her. She'd probably slap him. Too bad.

"On second thought, Caleb," Joe said, "never mind the water bed. This one's fine."

Liz smiled, looking flirtatiously at him. It was time for her to go to work on Mr. Stubborn. "I appreciate that, Joe. How about coming to my dressing room. I think I've got an Ace bandage for those weak knees of yours."

He had a good idea why she invited him, but he

followed her anyway. It wasn't often Liz asked him in for a visit, or that she asked anyone else for that matter. Joe shoved his hands into his rear pockets, admiring the sway of her hips as he kept two steps behind her. She'd been getting his goat and his attention for the better part of six months. If he said white, she said black. If he wanted to quit rehearsing, she'd insist on another run-through. If he wanted to leave early, she'd make him feel as if he were letting down the entire cast and crew and future generations of unborn fans.

"Let's dispense with the preliminaries," he said as they walked by his office. "I have it on good authority that you're going to try to talk me into doing that radio show with you."

She turned in her tracks, bumping into his chest. Thump. Her heart skipped a beat. Unwanted. Dangerous needs she'd lived too long without. Needs which Joe evoked whenever they were close. He put his arms around her and grinned.

"Let go of me. I hate when you do that, Joe."

"Hush up," he warned, chuckling at her discomfort.

"I will not," she retorted.

"Ah my sweet, do you want Shirley to think the lovebirds are arguing? You know what she'll do with *that* tidbit. Smile, darling." She extricated herself from his embrace and walked on twice as fast.

Once inside her dressing room, Liz closed the door and planted herself in front of Joe. "Okay, what gives? Why don't you want to do it with me?" She sounded exasperated.

"I *do* want to do it with you," he replied, smoothly.

"You know what I mean, dammit! Get your mind out of the—"

"Please." He held up a hand. "Don't spoil it."

Liz glared at him, but he was enjoying himself too much to stop baiting her. He was enjoying being closeted in her dressing room. He'd never seen legs like hers. They just kept going up until they met those gorgeous thighs. What was that song? Hipbone connected to the thighbone, thighbone connected to the—

"Joe, I'd appreciate an answer. It isn't every day one half of a successful couple turns down a plum offer like this. Since I'm the party of the second part I think I've got a right to know why you object."

"A make-believe successful couple, sweetheart. *Make-believe.* That's the operative word here." He sat down on the sofa, which was piled with scripts, books, magazines, and a squealing white toy poodle that jumped into his lap and began to lick his face.

"Herman, stop that," he said, pretending to muzzle the playful animal's snout. "Mommy's going to be very upset with us if we're not good little boys."

"Mommy's going to break your shiny black head if you don't tell me why you're so pigheaded stubborn," Liz muttered. She didn't usually bring Herman to work, but the producer had wanted a dog for one of the scenes.

Joe admired her nerve. "I happen to believe in the philosophy that some play for play's sake—is important. In short, my beauty, I've got plans for my vacation. As soon as we break for the summer hiatus I'm heading home to see my folks." His father's arthritis was acting up, and Joe wanted to see how he could help as well as hire more help for the family store.

Liz lost her patience. Annoyance surged through her. She was going to take a vacation too—a short one. And then she'd go back to work. She'd worked for years to be where she was in the business. Sure, there were days she wanted to chuck it all, but she had responsibilities. Life had dealt her a cut of the cards that severely limited her options. "You're serious, aren't you?"

Petting the dog, Joe viewed the play of emotions on her face. He couldn't quite figure out why this was so important to her. All he'd been able to glean about her private life was that after hours, Liz Davis became a woman of mystery. If she attended an awards show or a premiere she usually was escorted by her agent, a paunchy, middle-aged man. And there was never any gossip about her.

"Of course I'm serious," Joe replied. "I haven't been home to Colorado in ages. I've got a brother who's a doctor whom I miss. I'd like to see him and my sister-in-law and their family. Furthermore, I miss my folks. I miss Colorado Springs." Joe ducked as Herman vigorously licked his neck. "Who knows? One of these days I may just branch out, venture into another field. I'm not driven the way you are; besides, I fell into this part on a fluke anyhow."

Liz felt as if the breath had been pulled from her. Joe didn't know, couldn't know, that in large part her intense drive stemmed from the sheer terror of not being able to pay her bills otherwise. Her memories of the days she barely scrimped by were vivid. How luxurious it would be to be able to stay home if she chose, take a break for a year or so and enjoy her son Jason while he was still little. As much as she loved acting, the restrictions on her choices were often frustrating. She wished she had the leisure to take Jason on a real vacation this summer—not just a short jaunt to the Catskills before she headed to another job.

She plopped down on the sofa, her hands flopping by her sides. Despite her crushing disappointment, she understood his decision. She knew she shouldn't want to ruin his vacation, but she did. Together they were dynamite. They were unbeatable in the sweeps. Their battling relationship on the set fueled the sexual tension on camera. Seated with his long legs casually crossed at the ankles, his shirt open to reveal the light furring of hair on his chest, his eyes capturing hers with a deep blue intensity, he exuded an animal magnetism that was palpable.

"I understand you want to be with your folks," she said reluctantly.

"Liz, aren't you working long enough hours now? What do you do for a social life? You know what they say about all work and no play."

"I am going away too, for your information. For two weeks. I'd just hoped when I came back . . ." She shrugged her shoulders.

"Is this radio show that important to you?" he asked gently.

"Yes."

The ice princess doesn't volunteer any information or let anyone get too close, he thought.

"All right," he said, almost as a reflex. She got under his skin; there wasn't much he'd been able to do about it.

Until now, he thought cunningly.

"There might be a way I'd be willing to go along with this," he said carefully. "If you agree to fly out for the summer to Colorado, we'll tape the show from there." He saw the leap of interest in her eyes. "Provided our agents iron out the details. Those are my terms."

Liz considered the possibility of spending the remainder of the summer out West. There were plenty of horses in Colorado. Jason would learn to ride in the Catskills, then he'd have a chance to apply his skill in Colorado. It might just work out, she thought, warming to the idea. Jason would love it. The dry, bracing air and the grandeur of the Rockies would be a great alternative to the congested city. A bubble of excitement grew in her. She'd find a little rental, and with the extra money she'd finally pay off the last of her debts.

With an uncharacteristic display of affection, she threw her arms around Joe's neck, squeezing him in a hug. "Joe, you're wonderful! I knew you'd do it."

"Did you?" He frowned, but she was so happy she missed his meaning. Joe lifted her hand, and kissed her palm as himself, not the character he played, Dr. Hank Chalmers. "Suppose I ask you out on a date. What would you say to that?"

She slowly pulled her hand from his, still feeling the tingling effects of his lips and warm breath on her skin. She stepped out of the embrace she'd initiated. These weren't lines written for them by others and it wasn't part of a business arrangement. She thought of Jason, which made it easier to say what she had to.

"I'd say thank you for the invitation, but I never mix business and pleasure."

He shrugged. "I suppose I should be grateful to be put in the 'pleasure' category. Well, I guess I'll be on my way. We seem to have finished our business."

She nodded, but asked, "What kind of business is your dad in, Joe?"

"My parents own a toy store. When I was growing up I was the most popular kid in the class. Care to guess why?"

"Bribery." She laughed.

"Speaking of which," he said, "how about changing your mind? Call it a celebratory dinner for my being such a good sport and buckling under to your demands."

His boyish grin almost disarmed her. But she was afraid of succumbing to another type of demand. It would be different if she thought Joe would shake her hand at the end of the evening and not try to kiss her good night, or that she wouldn't gravitate to his arms, knowing what her insides felt like after he kissed her on camera. Having experienced his devastating technique, she might be foolish enough to let him lead her to the next experience: making love off camera. She owed Jason a mother with her head and heart devoted to him. Her heart was better off wrapped in lead.

"I'd better not."

Joe adopted a nonchalant air. "Then, dear lady, there isn't much left to say. We'll let our agents handle the particulars."

Liz didn't want him leaving this way. He'd agreed to her terms, only to be rebuffed. Couldn't she have said, Joe, I'm afraid I won't be able to stop myself, so it's better not to start? But how would he have reacted to *that* when he hadn't even proposed anything more than dinner?

"Don't go." She started to apologize, when her phone rang. Joe's hand was on the doorknob when her sudden scream brought him rushing to her side. Her face was drained of color. Liz spoke rapidly, her voice trembling. "When? Where are you, doctor? Which hospital? Yes, yes, of course, doctor. Please, don't wait. Do everything you can. I'll sign the necessary forms when I get there."

"What's wrong?" Joe asked.

"Joe," she said, her voice bordering on hysteria, "did you drive to work today?"

"Yes."

She grabbed her purse. "Please, I need a ride to Lenox General. It's an emergency."

"Let's go." He tucked his hand under her elbow, guiding her rapidly across the set. She paused to briefly tell the director she was leaving the set on a family emergency. He told her someone would take Herman home overnight. She was not to worry about anything. If necessary they'd write her character out of the script for a while. She and Joe had already shot their scene for the season finale.

On the ride to the hospital, she buried her face in her hands. Joe respected her privacy while she tried to get a grip on herself. Within minutes the car screeched to a halt in front of the emergency clinic.

"Go on in," Joe said. "I'll park the car and find you. What's the name of the patient?" Liz bolted out the door, shouting over her shoulder.

"Jason. My five-year-old little boy. My son, Jason Davis."

Joe was stunned. Liz had a son. His coworkers must have assumed he knew, and never mentioned it. Whatever the reason, it was a shock. "What about your husband?" he called after her. "Do you want me to phone him, let him know?"

"We're divorced. I have no idea where he is," she said as she flew toward the hospital's entry.

When he'd parked the car, Joe found Liz pacing up and down the waiting room. She jumped when he came to her side. He wrapped his arms around her, feeling her delicate bones through her clothes. She was shaking. Although he wanted to ask a million questions, he knew this wasn't the time.

"Joe," she sobbed, her eyes never leaving the door of the emergency room, where Jason was. "My son was hit by a car. He darted away from Fiona, my housekeeper, and ran into the street." The tears streamed down her face. "Oh Joe, it's his right leg. A closed fracture of the tibia. His little chubby leg. He has such cute dimples on his knees. Thank God it wasn't his kneecap. It should have been me instead. Why Jason?" she cried. "Jason shouldn't have to go through this."

Joe held her, letting her speak, letting the emotions pour out. Between her tears and gulps, she carried on about not being there for Jason. Joe had never seen Liz so vulnerable, and his heart went out to her. He gently wiped her tears away with his thumbs, then fished in his pocket for a clean handkerchief. He led her to a couch, where they sat and waited anxiously. She'd cry, then stop herself, then sit still in quiet desperation. Finally he couldn't stand her being in so much pain anymore. He cradled her head against his chest, wishing he had a magic wand to rewind the clock so the day could begin again with a different ending.

He learned Liz wasn't an ice princess after all. She was a frightened single parent, a mother with an injured child. "Liz honey, hold on. You'll see. Jason will be fine. I know it's hard to believe right now, but he'll pull through this. We'll both help him."

She shuddered, burrowing against his chest. "Will you help, Joe? I think I could use a friend."

"Shhh, you know I will." He found himself telling her about his family's home and invited her and Jason there as soon as the doctor gave the boy permission to fly.

When the doctor joined them, they learned Jason had come through the procedure well. The doctor assured Liz that Jason's leg should mend without complications. He'd have to spend a week in the hospital for observation to make sure there was no swelling. Liz eyed the doctor with suspicion, and Joe realized she was reserving judgment until she saw her son running around again.

She phoned their director, and told him she couldn't possibly leave Jason for a while. His response relieved her mind.

"Don't worry, Liz. As I said, we'll write your character out, saying she was called away on an emergency; that'll give Joe a couple of days off too. Tell him I said so. We've already shot the last show before the break, so no sweat."

Joe was pleased he'd be able to remain by Liz's side. He hoped he could convince her that Denver would be the perfect spot for Jason to recuperate. He made a mental note to phone his brother Tom, an orthopedic surgeon. With a doctor right in the family, how could Liz refuse? Then Joe thought of his father. If ever a man loved playing with little children, it was his dad. Jason might just prove to be the antidote his dad needed. He could keep his father company while they were both immobile for a while. His mother, he knew, would be delighted to hear the sounds of a little child in her house again. She was always pestering his sister-in-law Frances to leave six-year-old Mike and eight-year-old Janice whenever possible.

Joe thought fondly of the large family home, with spacious yard, the running spring, and the majestic, snowcapped Rockies in the distance. Deer often wandered onto the property. Raccoons were fearless, messing up the garbage pails unless they were tied down. The stream was alive with trout. It would be a fine place for a little boy to regain his strength, far better than the sidewalks of New York City. Jason would have friends close to his age for company. And Liz wouldn't be alone.

And neither would he.

The doctor returned later to check on a still sleeping Jason, reassuring Liz. "He's a lucky little boy. Had it been an open fracture, we could have had complications. But in this case he'll wear the long leg cast approximately four weeks, then a short leg cast for about another four. My suggestion is that you buy him a felt-tip pen. The more signatures the better, based on my experience with these kids."

Liz hung on to his every word, a worried expression on her face. How disappointed Jason would be when he learned their Catskill vacation plans would have to be canceled!

"Will he be able to fly?" Joe asked, taking her cold hand in his, kneading it with his warmth.

"I don't see why not," the doctor replied after Joe had explained their plans to go to Colorado. Joe added that his brother was an orthopedic surgeon. Liz remained silent, and Joe wasn't sure if she was going to agree to go, or give him a blistering later.

"I'll send him a report and Jason can have his physical therapy there, if you like," the doctor said. "In ten weeks he'll be running around as good as new. However, I'm going to keep him here for a week to watch that the swelling goes down. Strictly routine," he said. Liz unconsciously moved closer to Joe.

She remained at Jason's bedside until the nurses assured her the medication would keep him groggy until morning, and told her she should go home and rest. Joe forcibly, but gently, ushered her out of the room.

Liz learned from the police report, that neighbors who witnessed the accident said it was clear that neither the housekeeper nor the driver of the car had been negligent. Jason was greased lightning. He'd dashed off without warning, the terror-stricken Fiona screaming, running right behind him. Luckily, Jason was only grazed by the car. The force was just enough to cause the fracture.

Before leaving the hospital, Liz calmed the frightened housekeeper who had brought Jason in and sent her home for a few days. "There's nothing you can do, Fiona," she said wearily. "Get some rest; you need it."

When the two of them reached Liz's house, Joe told Liz he'd run down to the drugstore while she soaked in a hot tub. The doctor had ordered a mild sedative for her.

She adamantly refused. "Just aspirin, please. I don't want to be fuzzy-headed tomorrow."

"All right. But I'm substituting hot milk. Dr. Michaels' orders."

"Yes, doctor." She managed a weak smile. "The bath sounds heavenly."

While Liz bathed, Joe looked around her home. It kept his mind off imagining her naked in the tub. The apartment was cheerful. Apparently, Liz loved chintz. The sofa and two love seats were covered in it. The place was warm and comfortable —perfect for a young child. Children's books littered the tables, toys overflowed a chest in the corner near the television set, and sheet music about an itsy-bitsy spider was on the piano. He hadn't known Liz played.

Many framed pictures of mother and child adorned the piano. Joe peered at each, studying them. The child had intelligent eyes, the same brown-and-gold shade of his mother's, and a shock of blond hair. In one picture he proudly displayed colored Band-Aids on his arms and legs. Joe remembered how as a child he too had worn his wounds proudly.

He moseyed down the hall, poking his head into the bedrooms. There were two. Liz's was totally feminine, like its owner. Everything was white: frilled pillows, a lacy coverlet, white curtains. Pure as the driven snow, Joe thought. Not at all like the fire he knew beat beneath her cool exterior.

Joe smiled when he glanced in Jason's room. Jason was a Mickey Mouse buff. They had something in common. He'd also keep that in mind when buying the boy a present.

There was a second bathroom leading from the hall, with a domed skylight. He imagined the room was bright during the day. There were a lot of hanging plants all around the house, he noticed as he came back into the kitchen. Wait until Liz saw his mother's garden. His mother regularly planted her own herb and vegetable garden, which was bordered by an abundance of flowers.

He poured a glass of water, then went to the freezer for an ice cube. On the refrigerator door Jason's crayon drawings were held by Mickey Mouse magnets.

Refreshed from her bath, Liz came padding in, bundled from head to toe in a long white terry-cloth robe. Her face was scrubbed, her cheeks pink.

"Let's go into the living room," she said.

Liz looked refreshed—and relaxed. He couldn't help noticing how the lights made diamond patterns in her hair. *Dangerous thoughts.* Changing the subject, he asked, "Liz, does your ex-husband keep in touch with his son? Should you call him?"

Her face grew hard, her eyes flat. "No. He's never been interested in his son. It's his loss."

What a jerk, Joe thought, resenting the man who'd married Liz. Not to have been around to hold Jason, to help him take his first steps. No wonder she was so frantic when she heard Jason was hit by a car. No doubt she'd been facing crises for years all by herself.

Joe squeezed her hand in reassurance. "Make all gone with the milk, lady, and I promise to be here bright and early in the morning to take you to see Jason. I think I should meet him when he's awake, don't you?"

"Yes," Liz agreed. Her features softened as they rested on Joe. She'd really given him a hard time, and he couldn't have been nicer today. She wanted to make amends for her earlier behavior; she should let him off the hook.

"Joe, I can't thank you enough for seeing me through today. I know I got a little hysterical before, but I'm okay now." She reached for his hand. "I'm sorry I twisted your arm about the radio show. Forget it. I'm releasing you from any obligation. I know you agreed because I pressured you into it, but it isn't fair of me to intrude on your personal life when you want to be with your family. The trouble with you is that you're too nice a guy."

"Well, as I live and breathe," Joe said. "Is this Liz Davis welshing on a deal? How do you know I haven't thought it over? The fact is you're talking nonsense."

"You're sure?" she asked, a yawn escaped.

He nodded. "Get some beauty sleep. You're

bushed. Jason doesn't need to see his mom with bags under her eyes. And quit worrying. It'll all work out for the best." He gently tugged her braid. She was so exhausted, she couldn't keep her head up. "And think about making that trip to Denver."

Joe lay awake most of the night. "Bags," he mumbled to himself. How could he have said such a thing? When he stared into the mirror at his bloodshot eyes the next morning he realized he too had bags. He rubbed the stubble of his dark beard. With a towel riding low on his hips, he reached for the phone to set the wheels of change in motion. Liz called him stubborn. She didn't know the half of it. If she thought he was going to let her take Jason to a hotel while they were in Colorado, she was nuts. He wanted her under his family's roof, where he could keep tabs on her. Besides, now he knew how to handle her.

He hoped.

Two

He pointed.

She retaliated by scrunching up her nose.

"Eat."

"No."

"I suggest you change your mind."

"No."

"Eat or I won't drive you."

Liz's kitchen table was the battlefield. Joe had arrived promptly at seven-thirty with a sack of food in one hand, her dog Herman in another, and a broad smile on his matinee idol face. He nodded a cheery greeting to Liz, dropped the squirming poodle into her arms, took a more thorough look at her, shook his head, then brushed past her with a purposeful stride, disappearing into the kitchen, where she heard him banging open the cupboards. Liz let Herman down on the floor, and he promptly ran right back to Joe. He whined so pitifully for Joe to pick him up that Liz wondered what magic potion he'd slipped the pup. "Traitor," she mumbled.

Groggy, she remained rooted to her post near the door.

She'd drowsed fitfully during the night, with an eye on the digital clock, watching the minutes change. She'd been dressed since six-thirty, waiting impatiently for visiting hours to start. She paid scant attention to Joe's whistle drifting from the kitchen.

When his breakfast call failed to bring her running, Joe whistled his way back into the living room, Herman wiggling happily under one arm. "Now, Lizzy, we can't have Herman seeing you out of sorts, can we? A little food will fix you right up." Putting his other arm around her shoulders, he turned her in the opposite direction and marched her into the kitchen, where he pushed her into a seat. "Eat," he commanded. She responded by nervously shredding the napkin.

"I'm not hungry. Can we please go?"

Her appeal might have been to Joe, the walls, or to Herman, who sat in his begging position. Joe shoved a container of coffee and a container of cream in her direction.

"Dig in," he ordered, pointing to his ammunition: warm cinnamon buns, coffee, and a Vitamin C pill.

She glowered at him. Seeing him look so good this early in the morning put her out of sorts. Not to mention the way he filled out his clothes. Taut but not tight. As for her, she'd thrown on any old thing. Not her most spiffy duds.

She wore a pair of washed-out jeans with frayed

cuffs. The old, comfortable jeans that were perfect for playing or tumbling on the floor with Jason. The sneakers, scuffed and stained, had seen better days. The tops of her shoes were a motley shade of faded grape jelly and red dye, the latter gotten when Jason had turned over a bottle of soap-bubble liquid. The other stains were indistinguishable and grossly unmemorable. With it all, she wasn't about to discard a still serviceable pair of sneakers. You can take the girl out of the poor neighborhood, but thrifty habits die hard. She supposed she'd never change.

It had taken her only four or five seconds to do her hair. She'd piled it in a blond twist, secured it with a rubber band, and that was that. The way she figured it, her outfit didn't matter. After Joe dropped her off at the hospital she planned to remain in her son's room the entire day, leaving when he was asleep for the night. And surely Joe would leave quickly. He must have plans for the weekend. But right now she wanted to leave, not eat.

"Joe, I want to go to the hospital."

"It's not open."

Frustrated, Liz bit her lip. She should call a cab and be done with it; then he and Herman could eat all they wanted. "Don't be silly. Hospitals are always open. I'll just explain the circumstances."

"Not at this one," Joe replied complacently. He laid a glossy pamphlet on the table. It was the hospital's rules and regulations. "It's got firm visiting hours. Here, see for yourself."

"When did you get this?" Liz demanded.

"Yesterday, when I met with the admitting clerk

to process Jason's papers. You were occupied with him; I didn't think it necessary to tell you then, or you'd be upset for nothing. You know what a wreck you were. Jason's in good hands; you heard the doctor. He'll be out in a week, ready to start driving you crazy. Quit worrying so much—everything went like clockwork. There were no complications. Jason doesn't need to see you upset, or you'll transfer your anxiety to him."

"Now look here," she bristled. "I'm his mother. That qualifies me to—"

"To listen to reason and not get there like a wild woman. He's been through enough," Joe interrupted.

Liz's jaw dropped.

"You'll see Jason at ten o'clock. Nine-thirty if you eat like a good girl."

She eyed the food with the disdain she usually reserved for her co-star. "I never eat in the morning."

Joe broke off a piece of the bun. He gave a small amount to Herman, whose wagging tail shined the floor.

"That explains why you're such a pill," he went on. "You've been starving yourself. You shouldn't do that. It throws your electrolytes out of whack. Besides, mothers need their strength. If you won't eat for Jason, think about me. I don't want to hold a bag of bones on the set. There's nothing worse than making love to a bag of bones." He grinned, giving her bones an appreciative stare.

Liz fumed as she watched the rest of the bun disappear into his mouth. Three bites; Liz counted. As she watched in silence, he smacked his lips, slurped his coffee, and dug into the bag for another sweet roll. This time he slipped it to the dog. Herman was in heaven.

"Actually, you should probably eat a bowl of oat-bran cereal, eggs maybe three times a week, and fruit." He used a knife for emphasis. "Fruit's very good for you. The fiber, you know. Bananas, orange, or grapefruit. Drink lots of water. Keeps the system flowing. It might even retard wrinkles— not that you have any yet."

"Joe!" she exploded. "What are you, some kind of nutrition guru who tortures single mothers?" A nutrition guru who wolfed sugar buns at an ungodly hour of the morning, who looked terrific, and who spouted unasked for advice. It was more than she could swallow. Herman jumped, growled at her, then resumed his begging position at Joe's leg. Four-legged traitor!

Joe smiled unrepentantly. "Yes, dear." He covered her hand with his. It was warm and firm, she noticed before snatching hers away.

Flustered, she blurted out, "In the first place, I am not your 'dear.' You are simply kind enough to do me a favor. I've never been your 'dear' and we're not going to start now!"

Joe feigned a crestfallen expression. "Yesterday I was. Yesterday I was your dear. Yesterday you cried in my arms. Yesterday you clutched my hand. Yesterday you told me you couldn't make it without me." He buttered a piece of his roll.

She couldn't help wondering how he could sit there calmly stuffing his face. If she ate two sugared buns slathered with butter she'd gain five pounds.

Joe drained his coffee, reached into the sack for

another container, popped the lid, and took a long swallow. Liz had the impression Warden Joe Michaels intended to remain on duty until she did what he said. She'd never seen this side of his personality.

"Yesterday you begged me not to leave you," he said. "Yesterday I was most definitely your dear. Now you've hurt my feelings, Liz. I wouldn't do that if I were you." He bit into the bun.

Although she wanted to end this idiotic conversation, she couldn't help asking, "Why not?"

"I'll be happy to answer when half that roll disappears from the plate."

"Nuts!" she muttered under her breath, but she obediently snatched the cinnamon bun from her plate and took a vicious bite. The sensation of flavors rolled over her tongue. It was warm and gooey and surprisingly delicious. Without thinking, she minced another piece.

Joe chuckled inwardly, enjoying himself. He'd guessed she'd be too upset to fix herself breakfast. Her face was drawn with worry, and faint shadows were under her eyes. He could well imagine the night she'd spent.

The Liz he knew always put up a good front. Cheerful. Independent. A true professional who arrived promptly, always pulled her weight, rehearsed, did her scenes, and then retired to study or chat. The cast and the press adored her. In fact, the only person he'd ever seen her snub was Shirley Richards. "I can't forgive her for ruining Bob's career. She went after him with a hatchet," she'd said at the time.

Liz left the set promptly as soon as her duties

were over, presumably to live the life he'd learned about in the last twenty-four hours. She'd done a lot of ingenious covering of her tracks.

"Okay," she said, "it's half-gone; now answer."

"It's only right that you should ask," he said. His thoughts wandered to the day he'd discovered that Liz meant more to him than merely a fellow actor. He'd caught the fever after that. The Liz Davis fever, he'd dubbed it. "Take two aspirins and call me in the morning" didn't do the trick where she was concerned.

They'd spend hours shooting a love scene that had left him testy, unsatisfied, disgruntled, and generally not fit to live with. Until Jason's accident he'd been in a quandary as to what to do about it. . . .

"Liz, you know I'm a Method actor. But as good as I am, I've noticed I have a slight problem." He was pleased to notice she was giving him her undivided attention. It was all he could do to keep a straight face.

"What's your problem?" she asked.

"I'm getting to that." Joe leaned over to touch her hand reassuringly. "It's very hard for me to hold a woman in my arms and pretend we're in bed making love intensely unless I can use my imagination."

"I'm sure you've got an active imagination," she snapped. "May we leave now? I have a feeling this problem of yours might take all day."

He took a sip of coffee. "In a little while, Liz. There's no sense sitting outside waiting in the hospital parking lot when we can be all cozy and comfy in here. In the meantime, don't dawdle over your food. Eat up." Having no choice, she did.

His eyes twinkled with amusement. "There's a difference in degree, you know," he smiled meaningfully. "I'd like to explain what I think is the difference between making love intensely, arousing your whole being, exciting each and every nerve ending, and just making love, if I may?"

Liz gulped. "No, that's all right. It's a little early for a serious discussion."

She knew exactly what he was referring to, the louse. Amend that. The rat! He didn't have to explain a thing. He'd already showed her his version of intense lovemaking on the set, in front of the whole crew—at her expense! How dare he bring that up now, or even hint at it. Oh, the sneak!

She remembered that day all too clearly.

The scene called for Joe to slowly disrobe her by nudging the spaghetti straps of her lacy black negligee aside, drawing it down from her shoulders. His kisses became more passionate. The camera angle moved from her face to his bare upper torso, his rippling musculature, while she moaned, first on cue, then because she couldn't help herself.

How the pretense shifted to reality she never knew. Joe threw himself into his "Method acting" emoting until her lips were sucked swollen. In the beginning she feebly protested, tingling with sexual desire as he murmured in her ear not to break the tempo. Over and over Joe's lips and fingertips flowed over her sensitive skin, kissing her as if he couldn't get enough of her.

She'd blocked out her surroundings; she simply

lost touch with reality. Joe was her focus, her only focus.

Then, bingo! The worst scenario happened. Liz Davis, actress, forgot she was acting, looped her arms around his neck, and went to town.

It was an experience she never wanted to remember.

She took refuge in her dressing room, numb in the knowledge that for the first time in her acting career she had forgotten where she was. She and Joe could have been on display in a store window for all she cared at the time.

All her senses were magnetized by Joe, the taste and feel of him, the sheer strength of him. The worst part was that she'd loved it. When he laved her skin, the column of her neck, her collarbone and downward to the mounds of her breasts, she had become putty in his hands. True, the scene was written to be steamy, but who told Joe to add spice to it? Nothing in the script called for his thumb to skim over her breast, yet somehow it happened.

Out of the camera range to be sure, but it happened nevertheless. A flick. Then another flick. She should have stopped him, but she didn't. To her intense mortification her nipples reacted as if Joe's command was their very wish while her traitorous hips lifted of their own volition, fitting closer to his rock-hard body.

She preferred to forget the whole unfortunate episode. It was a cheap trick on Joe's part. Method, my foot! Only she couldn't forget she was equally guilty. It would be hypocritical to pretend she wasn't an active partner.

Compliments followed, along with applause.

Everyone said it was their best scene yet. And why not? It came humiliatingly close to the real thing. The ratings, which happened to be during the November sweeps, shot sky-high. So what did the writers do? They wrote more red hot scenes. When the ratings remained high, they wrote in still more!

Oh yes, she thought mulishly, she knew what kind of lovemaking Joe referred to, all right. And in her opinion, a true actor would never bring up such a slip of professionalism—certainly not now, in the intimacy of her kitchen. Joe shouldn't distract her from worrying about Jason. Especially since even after that awful day there were many times when Joe touched her that she almost lost control again, despite her good intentions.

After that, she'd steered clear of him when they weren't working. She'd give him a perfunctory greeting, raise her chin to a lofty position, and sail right past him, ready to go over her script. When they rehearsed she pretended nothing untoward had happened. They'd advise and critique each other's performance.

Except nothing was the same and she knew it.

Moreover, she knew he knew it.

She'd adopted a routine, reciting a mantra to keep calm and collected before falling into his arms for another scene. But the mantra was wearing thin.

She stirred from her reverie as Joe continued, "To do my best work I have to pretend it's real. If we fight, if I know you don't like me, that you're pretending to really like me, I simply can't emote.

Our fans will start catching on. And then down go our ratings. The kiss of death. You know the public's fickle. The writers will concentrate on other actors. You'll have less and less work, Liz. For myself, it doesn't matter," he added generously, after painting a financially morbid scenario.

She rolled her eyes and counted to ten.

"I'm simply thinking of you and Jason, the rent you pay on this place, which I assume from the neighborhood is quite expensive. Please eat your food. Did anyone ever tell you you dawdle? What a terrible example for Jason!"

She shook her head in disbelief. She didn't know whether to be deeply moved or to put her fist in his gorgeous face. "You're saying all this because I didn't want to eat breakfast?"

"Don't be silly." He wiggled his fingers in a gesture that urged her to consume the rest of her bun. "No. It's because you said not to call you dear."

"Not to call me dear?" She wasn't sure she heard correctly.

He took another bite of his bun. "Yes, you hurt my feelings. Hurry up," he said abruptly. "Herman and I are almost through."

She'd never figure out the male ego, if she lived to be a hundred. He was acting more like a child than Jason did. Except Joe had a driver's license and she still needed a ride to the hospital!

"By all means, call me dear," she said. Anything to get to the hospital.

He grinned, the glint in his eyes laser bright. "Thanks, dear, I shall. You may call me darling."

His timing was perfect. An unladylike amount

of coffee spilled from her lips. "In a pig's eye," she sputtered.

He handed her a fresh napkin. "Are you starting again?"

"Heaven forbid," she gasped.

"Then say it."

"Say what?"

"You know."

A cab could be at her place in fifteen minutes. Although she could drive, she refused to own a car in the city. She glanced up to find Joe intently watching her, a cajoling expression on his less-than-innocent face.

"Darling," she said. Her voice dripped with the same sugary coating oozing from the roll. "It's delicious. How can I possibly repay you?"

Joe sucked sugar topping from a finger, then wiped his hands with his napkin before getting up to wash. "You won't have to; tomorrow I'll fix bacon and eggs. It's my favorite. No, don't protest."

After a brief inspection of her plate, he added, "I know bacon's a bit high in cholesterol, but we'll zap it in the microwave between paper toweling. I'll get out most of the fat and all the nitrates. Every once in a while it's good for the soul to do what feels good. Lots of things besides food are good for the soul, don't you think?"

Liz's mouth had opened somewhere between the bacon and the nitrates being zapped in the microwave. It should have been funny, but it wasn't. A warning bell rang in her brain. He asked her to think. Think? How could she concentrate with Joe talking circles around her? His innuendos were so blatantly obvious they were ridiculous. And here she was so anxious to pay off her debts she'd asked him to do the radio show.

She sat up with a start. She'd promised to go to Colorado to tape the show. And now she'd be dragging a sick boy with her. Was it fair to Jason? And what was she letting herself in for? She'd be in enemy territory.

As if he knew her thoughts, Joe commented on the trip. "By the time our radio program begins we'll be familiar with each other, know each other's needs, satisfy each other's appetites. Familiarity makes for a better show, don't you think?"

"I think," she deadpanned, "familiarity breeds contempt."

He opened his palms in a gesture of defeat, smiling with a hint of sadness, a tragic figure shaking his head.

"Liz, Liz, Liz, what am I going to do with you? You're a tough woman. Nevertheless, you've finished your food, and I always keep my promises. Okay, let's go. Where's your deck of cards?"

"Cards?" She glanced at her empty plate. While he'd rattled on, she'd unwittingly finished every crumb of her cinnamon bun and drank all her coffee. She tossed the paper plates into the garbage pail, refusing to acknowledge she'd eaten the crumbs too. "You want to play cards. Now?"

"No, silly. If I'm going to entertain Jason I have to show him my magic card tricks. I've got the other stuff in the car. We'll spend a pleasant day."

Her head whipped around. Even though Stan said Joe had no scenes today or tomorrow, she never for a moment thought Joe intended to spend the *whole* day with her. "You're planning on staying at the hospital with us all day?"

"What did you expect?" he said with a trace of imperial scorn. "I can't leave you alone with Jason. There's no telling what trouble you might get into in your mental state. You heard Stan yesterday. I'm to stick to you like glue until I think it's safe to leave you."

"That's not what he meant," she protested, imagining endless platters of food being shoved at her.

"You have your interpretation," he said loftily, "I have mine. Shall we go or do you intend to waste more time?"

Stunned, Liz realized she hadn't the foggiest notion what to expect where Joe Michaels was concerned. He had more moves than a snake in the grass. A smart-as-a-whip, Phi Beta Kappa, snake in the grass. But a snake nevertheless. "I'll get the cards. Will one deck do?"

He tucked his hand under her elbow, led her into the living room, gave her a gentle hug, then patted her rump. "Two's better, dear. Remember to say darling. You forgot that time, but I forgive you."

Liz was silent on the drive to the hospital. Afraid of how she'd find Jason, she chewed on her bottom lip. How was she going to keep her active child occupied for the entire recuperative period? How was she going to tell him that there would be no Catskill vacation? Most important, was she making the right decision about taking him to Colorado? Maybe he'd be better off at home? Maybe *she'd* be better off at home. Jason and Joe still hadn't met. Suppose they didn't get along? Joe mentioned coming from a large family. How would they feel about two strangers in their midst?

"Joe, about Colorado," she began, nervous with indecision. "Perhaps now isn't the time, in view of all that's happened."

"Don't be silly. There couldn't be a better time. Anyway, it's all set. You've nothing to worry about, dear. I called my agent, Harvey Taylor, last night. He's finalizing the deal today with your agent—who I must say is delighted for you." He pressed her hand reassuringly, making her feel guilty for her suspicions. Why couldn't she take him at face value?

"Thank you," she murmured, aware she was increasingly beholden to Joe. She wasn't certain she liked feeling obligated. There never was a debt that didn't need repaying, her father had always said.

When Joe parked the car she made a dead run for the entrance. Luckily, he found a nearby parking space. He caught up with her at the elevator.

One of the nurses did a double take when she saw Joe. First she blushed, then she stammered a greeting. Another nurse asked for his autograph. No one seemed to notice Liz. Liz caught the looks of adoration on the women's faces. Joe graciously signed autographs, chatting with the women while Liz caught snatches of a whispered conversation between other nurses who probably thought she couldn't hear.

"Who is she?" one asked. Someone must have told her, because the response was a stage-whispered disbelief.

"You're kidding! I don't believe it! She's a lot prettier on TV."

"Shhh. She's upset; she's not wearing makeup. That must count for something."

"True, but still, you'd think she'd take better care of how she looks in public; I mean, she's all right, but who expected her to look so normal. Like us. That's not the way a star should look. Do you think those two've got something going on the side? I mean, he's here with her and it is pretty early."

"Let's go." Irked, Liz tugged on Joe's sleeve, and dragged him into the elevator. She didn't care to hear how plain she was or the nurses' whispered responses. So much for her loyal fans!

Holding his bag of surprise goodies for Jason in one hand, Joe held his finger on the *Door Open* button. Pouring on the charm, he called out, "Bye, ladies. Catch you later; maybe we'll have time for a cup of coffee."

"Joe, close the damn door!"

He grinned down at her. Liz was fuming. "Nice ladies, don't you think?" he said.

Liz glared at him, ready to belt him in his smiling puss for his chivalry. Those women acted as if she were chopped liver. She was a star too, for goodness' sake! How could Joe invite them for coffee after hearing their catty remarks?

She resented the way he looked at them, the way they swooned when they looked at him, gushingly hanging on to his every dopey word, as if they couldn't get enough of him. Morosely, her glance passed over her own ratty attire. So what? she fumed, thinking of her son waiting for her upstairs. Her attire was appropriate for the occasion. This was her private life, not her public one.

Joe's knuckles grazed her cheek. If looks could kill, he thought happily, he'd be a dead duck. Poor Liz. She was having a terrible time trying to decide whether to act grateful to him for coming with her or to kick him in the shins for flirting with the nurses. Which he'd done to get her goat.

"Don't be hurt, dear. I don't think you're prettier on TV." He slid a proprietary glance at her. Actually, he thought she was a darn sight prettier off camera, where her natural beauty was unrestricted by costumes and stage makeup, but he wasn't about to tell her that. What he wanted from her would take time. In the meantime, the best approach in handling his temperamental costar was slow and easy.

"You don't?" Liz's voice raised in reaction to the unexpected compliment.

"Uh-uh," he replied. "You look the same off and on."

Three

Liz stepped out of the elevator and was immediately assaulted by the sights and smells of the medical world. Doctors, nurses, attendants, and aides carried on their duties while loudspeakers paged physicians. It made her shiver.

Joe laced his fingers through hers, steadying her, giving her time to calm down. They walked around a mobile food cart, where breakfast trays were being stacked, waiting to be returned to the food-service area. One of the nurses came out of a room, posting a chart on the door.

She smiled in recognition. "Hello, you're Jason Davis's mother, aren't you?" Liz nodded. "I was on duty yesterday, but I wasn't assigned to your son until today."

"Is he all right?" Liz's fingers tightened automatically around Joe's.

"He's fine," the nurse said brightly. "I need to take Jason's temperature and vital signs before you go in. Sometimes these little ones get too excited if they see their parents. Give me about three minutes, then come on in. By the way, his doctor's already been by to see him this morning."

Joe was glad for the delay. "Liz, before you see Jason, try to remember that none of this was your fault. It's a waste of energy to blame yourself."

Despite her fatigue, she wondered if she was transparent—or was Joe a mind reader in addition to being a magician? She'd spent five years keeping her nose to the grindstone, auditioning, taking any and every job—not really out of a desire for a career as much as wanting to give Jason everything possible. Since the horrible phone call she'd been consumed with feelings of recriminations. "How did you know?" she stammered, her shoulders sagging.

"It's written all over your face," he told her.

Liz was stunned.

He put his arms around her, drawing her to his chest. All her defenses were down. This was the real Liz Davis, the woman the public didn't see. He worried about her. She seemed so fragile. "Think of it this way: It's Jason's second day and he's only here for a week—less now, if you subtract the hours since midnight." He smiled down at her.

Liz welcomed his outstretched arms, clinging to him, accepting the solace he freely offered. For once it was good not to be independent, good to share with another adult. Strange that it should be Joe, the last man she'd ever guessed would be there for her.

"I can't help feeling guilty," she said. "You would too if you were in my place."

He searched her gold-flecked eyes. "No I wouldn't," he argued, soothing her back with a gentle massage. "Neither should you. Accidents happen. You're an intelligent woman—you know all this as well as I do."

Her eyes glittered with tears. Sniffling, she fished in her purse for a tissue, then blew her nose. "No I don't," she said bitterly. "This was an unnecessary accident. If I were home where I belonged, raising my child, this never would have happened; Jason wouldn't be here. I cheated him by going to work right after he was born; I'm still cheating him. Fiona spends more time with him than I do. I missed his first word, didn't see him take his first step." She held up her hand, preventing Joe from speaking.

"Please, if you're about to mention 'quality time' to me, I'll scream. As far as I'm concerned, that odious phrase is a platitude coined by magazine editors and spouted by psychologists and businesspeople whose job it is to make parents feel less guilty. In my case it doesn't work." She broke away from him and strode down the hall.

He caught up with her. "Liz, you did what you had to do. You know how many women are in the work force today; even with two incomes, it's tough making ends meet. Are you condemning all of those women too?"

She tossed her head. If her ex were here right now, she'd cheerfully wring his neck. "Joe, what others choose to do is their business, but what you're saying doesn't change my feelings. The man I married was more immature than my son. He traveled a lot on business. My competition wasn't another woman—it was the free life on the road. It's a situation I'd never put myself in again! I never wanted to leave my baby, but I had to. I made a promise to myself to protect Jason, to give him the best life I can. Look where my promise got him. I wasn't where I should have been and my son was hurt."

From that short speech Joe learned more about Liz than he had from all the scenes he'd played opposite her. She didn't need sympathy now, she needed strength. His. His voice was calm, his determination matching hers. "When Jason goes to school are you planning on sitting in class with him all day?"

"Of course not," she huffed. "He attends nursery school."

"What about regular school, where the kids are older, tougher. Suppose he falls off the jungle-gym bars? Or gets hurt wrestling? Or gets into a fight with another child? Kids get injured in school all the time."

"That's different." She pushed a strand of hair away from her mouth, her eyes on Jason's door to see if the nurse was coming out.

"How?" Joe asked.

His logic annoyed her. She operated on emotion. Emotion based on experience, while he was operating on theory and no experience. "It's just different, that's all. Look, I don't care to discuss this. You're not a parent, so you can't know what I'm feeling."

He let that go for the moment. If she weren't upset he doubted she'd have made that remark. As actors they earned their living transmitting emotions, were sensitively attuned to them, understood them.

"I thought you loved acting."

She met his gaze levelly. "If I had my druthers you can bet your bottom dollar I'd be home with my baby until he went to school. I may love acting, but I *LOVE* Jason. To me the two loves don't have the same weight. I don't fault any mother who makes day-care arrangements for her child so she can work; this is the age of choice. This is mine—if I had one, which I don't. Just thank your lucky stars this isn't happening to your child. When you marry you'll know what I mean."

"Isn't that a bit like suggesting that unless I've committed a murder I shouldn't try writing a murder mystery? For your information, I've seen plenty of cuts, bruises, sprains, and breaks in my time. Don't forget, I'm a professional uncle. Not only that, but I went through a similar situation when I was about Jason's age. That ought to qualify me for something."

Liz was contrite. She'd accepted his generosity, then lashed out at him. "I'm sorry, Joe. I guess I'm just cracking under the tension. I shouldn't be taking my problems out on you."

The paging system clicked on. A woman's bland voice called for one of the fifth-floor residents to pick up the phone for an urgent message. Liz began walking to Jason's room. She refused to wait any longer.

Joe linked his arm with hers, slowing her down. "Hey, you're only human."

Liz decided this was a good time to change the subject. "Joe, if Jason isn't polite to you or if he's cranky, please forgive him. He's used to me or Fiona. This place might be throwing him for a loop."

Not as much as it was throwing his mother, Joe added silently. From just outside his room they heard Jason complaining that he didn't want to use the bedpan.

"It's for babies," he cried. "I'm a big boy!"

Liz had barely stepped inside before Jason, spying an ally, shouted, "Mommy! I waited for you. How's Herman? Does he miss me?" He shoved aside the pad of paper and the crayons on his lap. The nurse glanced up. She put down the empty pan.

"Sorry it's taking so long, but Jason and I are working out a compromise. He gets to keep the crayons, provided—"

Liz nodded. "Herman's fine, sweetheart. He sends his love. So does Fiona." She breathed a sigh of relief. Bedpans she could handle. At least Jason's coloring looked good. She hugged and kissed him, careful not to disturb his leg. Her eyes did a quick mother's thorough search. Her son was all in one piece. He appeared none the worse for his experience. Now if only her stomach would stop housing butterflies, she might make it through the day.

"I don't want to use the bedpan. It's too cold," Jason whined, spitting the thermometer out of his mouth to make his point. He hadn't yet noticed Joe, whose shoulders shook in silent mirth. He agreed with Jason completely.

In person the youngster showed an even stronger resemblance to Liz than in pictures. They had the same tiger eyes and blond hair coloring, and it was clear Jason possessed the same dig-in determination as his mother.

Jason patted the bed, urging his mother to sit down, then caught a glimpse of the tall stranger in the doorway. The child's mouth immediately turned downward. He'd had enough of physicians for the day. Two had examined him an hour ago. They had promised not to give him a needle, but this man was under a cloud of suspicion. Why was he here?

He was the enemy.

"Mommy," Jason whispered in her ear. "Tell the doctor to go away. I'll be good."

Liz turned to Joe, a look of pained entreaty in her eyes. It broke her heart to hear Jason plead that he'd be good. "You are good, honey. You're wonderful."

"Who's that man?" Jason asked from where he'd hidden his face in her neck. Joe held his finger to his mouth, restraining Liz from introducing them. How or if the boy accepted him was the key to his plans.

With a great flourish he noisily dug into his black garbage sack, ruffling the sides and retrieving a collection of soap-bubble bottles, a large hoop, a cocktail straw, a small circle, and a small tube of petroleum jelly. Alerted to something interesting, Jason craned his head over his mother's arm. He understood soap bubbles a lot better than needles.

Joe dove into the bag again, taking out several plastic soup bowls. He poured a generous amount of the various colors of liquid into each dish. The nurse swiftly slipped a new thermometer between Jason's lips. Joe greased the hoop with the salve, then dipped the small circle into the clear liquid. Joe transferred the liquid from the wand to the larger hoop. He swept the circle upward, magically producing a huge bubble, the size of a child's beanbag seat. Enthralled, Jason sat mesmerized, his mouth clamped around the thermometer, clutching his mother's hand.

Liz blessed Joe for his theatrical entrance. It was the perfect touch. Joe dipped the wand into a red liquid. In a flash he pricked the giant bubble, to the gasps of his audience. The bubble remained intact; magically, the red bubble appeared inside the larger one. Repeating this process, the blue-and-green bubbles were transferred to the larger one. Joe sent the giant multicolored bubble to Jason with a wave of his hand. Jason squealed his delight while the two women clapped. They groaned as the bubble fell to the floor and disappeared.

But Joe wasn't through. He whipped out the deck of cards Liz had given him. His audience was caught up in the magic as Joe shuffled the deck, flashing the ace of spades. Jason started to speak, but Joe shook his head, shushing him with a look as he shuffled the deck. Liz had never seen her son so wide-eyed. Using mime and hand signals, Joe ordered Jason to tap the deck with a magic wand. With a flourish Joe produced the card from the deck.

Jason couldn't stand it anymore. "How did you do that?" he squealed. The nurse salvaged the thermometer.

Joe shrugged noncommittally. "Can't tell."

"Why not?"

"Cause you're not my official helper." Joe pulled up a chair. From his pocket he brought out a large round badge with the words *Official Helper.* "Only helpers know the secrets. It's a strict magician's rule. Right, dear?" He turned to Liz for confirmation, but she was so dumbfounded that he'd called her dear in front of Jason that she could only nod. Why was he doing that?

Determined to own the official badge, Jason declared, "I want to be your helper."

Joe cocked his head. "Ask your mom if you can be my official helper. If she says yes, then I'll show you how I did it. If not, it's been nice knowing you, kid." He pretended to leave.

Jason tugged Liz's arm. "Please, Mommy. Please let me be the magician's helper."

Liz whispered in Jason's ear.

"No! I'm not going to use that pot. I hate it. It's for babies."

Joe gave the high sign to the nurse. They walked to the door. "When will he be able to use the bathroom?"

"Soon." She wasn't making deals.

Joe came to the bed, pulled up a chair, and sat down. "Jason— "

"How do you know my name?"

Joe's tone to Jason was pleasant, but when he looked at Liz his eyes were disapproving. "Magic— but if you want the truth, your mother told me. Dear, may I speak to you a minute, please?"

Reluctantly, Liz trotted after him. "That was a cheap shot," Joe said bluntly. He wore a mutinous look.

Liz took his chastisement without interrupting, while she considered whether or not to ask him about the "dear" business. She readily admitted to herself she shouldn't have tried to bribe Jason by using Joe's request for a helper. It made Joe look like the heavy after he'd knocked himself out entertaining Jason.

"I'm not handling this well, I know. I'm sorry; it's just that I'm worried about him. You know why the nurse was in there so long."

"Liz, sooner or later Jason would have given in. He'd have had to."

She waited a long moment before meeting his eyes. The corridor smelled of antiseptic. "I know." Several youngsters passed by, their parents alongside them. She smiled at them.

Joe followed her gaze, felt her tense, then said, "Forget it. I'll see what I can do to salvage this introduction."

Liz nodded. She was grateful he didn't walk out of the room and leave her on her own to face her belligerent child. She certainly deserved it. Any child psychologist would have faulted her actions. Mistakes and guilt, she thought morosely, were her middle name.

Joe approached the bed. "Jason, your mother and I have held a conference. If you agree to do what the nurse asks, I promise you you'll be my helper. Mommy only wants what's best for you."

Jason heard only that he was to be Joe's helper. His face was wreathed in smiles. They shook hands to formally seal the pact. Then Joe pinned the large badge-type button on Jason's pajama top.

"Yeah!" Jason cried happily.

Jason ignored his mother for the next three hours as he watched Joe, enthralled. Finally his eyes sagged. He'd used the bedpan for Joe, flatly refusing his mother's help. When he fell asleep in the middle of a yawn, the deck of cards was strewn across his stomach.

Liz stroked his forehead. He was cool, mending just as the doctor had assured her he would. A week. No, she corrected herself. Less than a week. Six days more. How does Joe do it? she wondered. Jason was putty in his hands, his own small fingers earnestly trying to mimic those of Joe's. She'd never seen Jason so attentive.

"Let's get something to eat," Joe said. "I'm hungry and I'm parched. Between the two of you I've never talked so much in my life." He picked up the deck of cards, replacing them in the box.

"You go," Liz said, shaking her head. "I'll stay here in case he needs me."

Joe lifted her bodily off the chair. "Wrong, dear. This is nap time for Jason, feeding time for us. If you don't eat you'll lose too much weight. Your fans will think you're anorexic. The station will be flooded with mail, which they'll read first and which you'll have to answer. Being the nice guy I am, I'll have to help you. I hate to write letters, unless they're love letters. So march, dear. You can think about what you're going to eat on the way down."

On cue, Liz's stomach rumbled. "Thank you for the applause," Joe added smugly.

In the packed elevator Joe unobtrusively winked at her. When she glared at him, she caught the devilish look on his face; by the time they emerged,

Liz was laughing and shaking her head. There were many facets to Joe. She remembered his face as he had entertained Jason, watching Jason for signs of fatigue, gauging how much to teach the boy, praising him when he mastered even a small portion of a trick, always offering encouragement, then promising Jason to buy him his very own magician's starter kit.

"How did you do it, Joe?"

"What?"

"Get my son to do whatever you wanted."

He grinned at her, leering in a way that made her sorry she'd asked. Being around Joe was like being around a tinderbox. She never knew what she'd say to set him off.

"It's my basic charm. I'm lovable. Women, children, and dogs can't resist me. Tomorrow we'll bring the kid a pastrami sandwich with pickle."

"We will not!" she retorted, a smile creasing her face. "Who's the one who was so worried about cholesterol today? Mmmmm?"

The air outside was clean and pure, all traces of the smog that had blanketed the city the previous week gone. A bright blue sky formed a vivid curtain for a skywriter in a small plane. Joe thrust his hands in his pockets, watching.

"Well, can you beat that. He's advertising a weekend in the Poconos at a honeymoon hotel. Wanna go?"

Liz knew he was kidding, but it was still a relief to be silly after what she'd been through. She suspected Joe's leering was part of a grand design to ease her tension. Whatever it was, she was eternally grateful for his presence.

They found a luncheonette a few blocks away and eased their way down the narrow aisle to a rear booth. As the waitress handed them their menus she lingered over Joe, fussing with his napkin and table setting. Liz wondered if there was a special woman in Joe's life. There must be. She suspected a man who enjoyed life as much as Joe did rarely enjoyed it alone. She was fully aware of the admiring glances he'd received from women as they'd emerged from the hospital. She'd seen his effect on the women on the set, but she hadn't been with him in public before.

Tomorrow she'd dress up. That is, if Joe planned on coming again; if not, she'd wear any old comfortable thing. She lifted her eyes from the menu, realizing that Joe was quietly watching her.

"So, what shall we eat? Chateaubriand for two? Duck a l'orange? I'm told they do a wonderful asparagus vinaigrette. For dessert we can order strawberry mousse pears on creme Anglaise."

She giggled at the waitress. "I'll have one of everything he said."

They ordered two ham on rye sandwiches, light on the mustard, and iced tea.

When the waitress left, Liz said softly, "Thanks, Joe. I'm okay now."

·He peered at her. "Darling," he said, switching moods like a chameleon. "You forgot to call me darling."

Liz caught her breath at the burning look in his eyes. All traces of humor vanished. Liz found his hand covering hers; she automatically responded, giving it a gentle squeeze. They might have been alone on a desert island, with only the swaying palm trees, the surf, and the music in their hearts for accompaniment. The blaring jukebox music faded as their gazes locked and held. The orders, shouted across the counter by busy waitresses, faded along with the faces of the luncheon crowd. It was as if the two of them were viewing one another for the first time and were enormously pleased by what they saw. And it was as if each of the kisses they'd shared on camera were, magically, ones they'd shared in private.

Liz snapped out of her trance when the waitress brought the food and set it before them.

"Eat up," Joe said.

Had she imagined his look of desire? Had all his attention simply been his way of keeping her occupied? She gave herself a mental shrug. Surely it hadn't meant anything. If it had, surely Joe would have said something, given a hint. Something.

She took a bite of her sandwich, asking cautiously, "Joe, how is it you've never married?"

"How do you know I haven't?"

Her stomach thudded. She settled herself onto the seat, knowing she'd never really considered whether he was or had been married. She'd been so wrapped up in her life she'd never considered his. "Are you? Have you?"

He reached for the mustard, pleased by her interest. "No." He sipped his iced tea. "Although I must say it's my mother's dearest wish. Whenever I'm home she troops in all the marriageable girls in the state. Unfortunately, Mom belongs to a lot of clubs, and her friends know a lot of eligible women. Her biggest fear is that I'll come to no good in the big bad city. I love my mother, but at my age it's a bit much. It's her only fault; the rest of her is perfection. Anyway, with you and Jason there, she's hardly likely to bring in the girls."

"In other words, I'm sort of an insurance plan," Liz said dryly.

"Don't be ridiculous. Marriage is fine for people who know what they want. You, for instance. You're the marrying kind."

"You'd rather play," Liz said disapprovingly.

"No, only as long as I'm a bachelor. Hey, it's a free world," Joe responded. "I'm exercising my free will."

The food didn't taste as good as she thought it had. She held the half-sandwich limply, then put it down on her plate.

"Joe, tell me more about your family."

He smiled. "I grew up in a large house my parents built to resemble a farmhouse. It's set on a grassy knoll, in a clearing in what was once a forest. It's not exactly Tara, but the house was large enough to rattle around in and fight with my brother without my mother and dad finding out—most of the time. Dad owns a toy store in town, but he's got a streak of the outdoorsman in him. He reads westerns and biographies of the mountain men. Enough yet?"

She shook her head no, eager to know more.

"Okay," he said. "My brother and I did all the usual things, except we did them surrounded by the Rocky Mountains, with deer roaming in our yard and raccoons knocking over the garbage pails, even when we tied the barrels down. We hiked and fished in our stream. There's nothing to match the taste of fresh fish. What about you? Spare me the press-release folderol. I already know you lived in Philadelphia"

"Nothing so dramatic." She told him about growing up there, about her father being gone at odd hours as his shifts changed, about her mother, with whom she was very close. "Tell me about your schooling," she said to Joe.

"In a minute. Where are your parents now?"

"They're gone," she said sadly. "Go on with your story," she prompted.

So you don't have to go on with yours. Not only do you have major responsibilities, but you have no one to share them with, he thought.

"School was pretty much the same as anywhere. One of my teachers believed in holding class outside when the weather permitted, winter or summer. We'd go on nature hunts, poking around in the snow for whatever the teacher asked us to try to find. In the spring we'd listen to the orchestral spring thaw as the water cascaded down the mountains. We'd lay on the grass while she read Shakespeare to us. She's the reason I love to read. It was a good place to grow up."

Liz envied him. Her Philadelphia school had high wire gates and was surrounded on three sides by concrete walls. There was graffiti smeared on the building. No sooner was it scrubbed off than it appeared again. Not raccoons, but bullies, many of them dropouts, overturned trash barrels.

"It sounds ideal," she said. "especially since your mother was there for you."

Too late, Joe realized he should have kept his mouth shut. Liz had a one-track mind, and he knew exactly which track it was on: motherhood guilt. At least he'd made all the arrangements for the summer. Liz could relax with her son. He'd phoned home last night, telling his parents about the radio show.

"By all means, Joe, invite them to stay here with us," his mother had said. "It'll be fun, break the boredom for Dad. Make sure to tell Liz she and Jason are welcome. I'll call in a few days to tell her myself."

"Tell me about your brother," Liz requested.

Joe chuckled. "Tom's two years older than I am. He flies a plane for relaxation, wanted to be a doctor from the time I can remember. He was a contradiction in terms—a serious student, yet a social animal until he met Frances. You'll like her. Now Tom's Mr. Settled: home, hearth, pipe, and slippers."

Liz relaxed against the back of the booth. His eyes were on her, and she thought them bluer than any she'd ever seen before. "And you?" she asked softly, wanting to know more about him. "Were you a social animal too?"

Joe sidestepped her question. "I never kiss and tell," he said mildly. "Suffice it to say I've had fun. I still do."

His words sunk in. "In other words, mind my own business."

If he could have had one wish it would have been to kiss the pout off Liz's lips right there and then. He hated to leave her last night. Events were happening he couldn't control. Dressed in her jeans, with only faint traces of makeup, her hair drawn back youthfully, she looked eager, happy, hanging on to his every word.

"Liz, if we were lovers, would you want me to go around telling people? Intimacy is a private affair."

Liz refused to rise to the bait. She pointed to her watch. "I think it's time we were getting back. You stay if you want to, Joe; I'm anxious to see if Jason's awake."

Joe held her gaze until she blushed. A smile formed on his lips. His voice was low and husky. "Chicken."

Her mouth fell open.

She preceded him out the door. It amazed and infuriated her that earlier she'd dwelled on the image of them as lovers. And now Joe had all but told her his love life was off limits, that it was active, that he had no intention of getting married.

Joe spent the afternoon much the same way he spent the morning, entertaining Jason. Liz fell asleep in the chair, waking up when she heard Jason excitedly say, "You'll really play football with me when my leg gets better?"

"Absolutely."

"And we'll go fishing?"

"You know it, sport. I'll even show you how to bait your own hook."

"And we'll play Nintendo games?"

"Without missing a day."

Liz slowly opened her eyes, listening to their conversation. Yawning, she stretched her arms above her head to come half-awake.

"Well, well, dear's finally decided to wake up," Joe grinned.

Liz rubbed her eyes. "Mmmmm. How long was I out?"

"I don't know, dear." Joe nudged Jason. "What would you say, partner?"

Jason caught Joe's use of the strange name for his mother. "Why do you call Mommy dear?" Jason asked.

Joe ruffled Jason's hair. "She is a dear, isn't she? Besides, she calls me darling," he said simply.

Liz frowned at him. What nonsense was Joe starting now?

Joe lazily uncrossed his legs. Liz couldn't pull her eyes away from his steady gaze. "That's a good name for her, don't you think?"

Jason wasn't sure. He'd never heard a man call his mother anything but Ms. Davis or Liz. His fingers worked the edge of the blanket. "Dear, huh?" His voice sounded doubtful.

"Dear," Joe confirmed. Liz tried and failed to get his attention. She wanted him to stop.

"And Mommy calls you darling?" Jason persisted.

Liz coughed. "Not all the time," she said quickly. Part of her wanted to choke Joe; the other part of her was curious to see how Jason handled this information. He'd never seen her with men other than his uncles, her agent, and people associated with the business.

"Is D your favorite letter?" Jason queried. "Is that why you want Mommy to call you darling?"

"Among other reasons," Joe answered cautiously. The two had spent all day getting to know one another. While Liz slept he'd told Jason all about his home in Colorado Springs. He told him about his six-year-old nephew Mike and his eight-year-old niece Janice, who were anxious to meet him. He saved the best for last, telling Jason that his father owned a toy store.

"Is D your favorite letter, Joe?" Jason repeated now.

"I think you might say that," Joe answered prudently.

Jason nodded. "Am I your helper? Truly?"

Joe picked up his hand. "Truly. You're the best."

"And D is your favorite letter, right?"

"Pretty much," Joe said, equally curious to see where this was leading.

"Mommy's dear and you're darling right."

Joe nodded.

Suddenly Jason's face lit up. He smiled broadly. "Good. Then I'm playing the D game too. I'm going to call you Daddy and you can call me Doug. How's that?"

Liz gasped. Her hand flew to her mouth, her eyes from Jason to Joe. For once Joe was speechless. Jason sealed the pact: Pulling Joe to him, he planted a juicy kiss on his cheek, oblivious to the adults shock.

Joe reacted by losing his heart to a five-year-old boy who wanted a father of his own, who he knew was trying to please him in any way he could. Swallowing the lump in his throat, he said, "Fine, Doug."

Happy and tired, Jason flopped back on his pillow. It had been a terrific day after all. "Thanks, Daddy. This beats a vacation in the Catskills, right, mom?"

An unexpected warmth spread from the top of Joe's head to the tips of his toes. He hadn't planned this. All he'd wanted to do was to lighten up a difficult situation for Liz and her child. He wanted the mother in a purely male way, yet being with Jason subtly altered everything. Joe couldn't help wondering if this warm glow was how fathers felt when thinking about their sons.

"What have you got to say about all this, dear?" Joe asked, catching the horrified look on Liz's face.

She snapped to attention at his question. The nerve of the man. Oh she had plenty to say, all right! None of it complimentary. What in the world did Joe think he was doing, allowing it to go this far. Jason would forget this had started out as a game. He'd learn to call Joe Daddy. Then what? Couldn't Joe see the child hero-worshipped him?

Jason watched her intently. Not wanting to upset him, she smiled through gritted teeth. "Why don't we wait until we get out of here?"

A little voice chirped, "Say darling to Joe, Mommy."

Joe grinned. "You heard your son; I had nothing to do with this."

Not much!

"Go ahead, Mommy. It's your turn."

She sent Joe a frosty look.

"Darling," she snarled.

Four

As he started the car, Joe glanced over at Liz. A man had to be nuts to be thinking about making love to a woman who was furious with him, yet that was exactly what was on his mind. She was beautiful. The stars were out and there was a full moon illuminating her high cheekbones. It was a perfect night for romance. Except that it was taboo. Taboo to be dreaming about stroking Liz's bare skin, of dropping kisses along her spine, of holding her close. Of kissing her fears away until all she thought about was him.

A lot of good these fantasies did him. Her *Off Limits* protective shield was on as surely as if it were made of metal. She was sealed as close to the passenger side window as she could manage. Clearly he was a persona non grata for encouraging Jason.

Liz stewed. She knew she had to stop this charade now; it had all the earmarks of becoming next to impossible to halt. But it wasn't fair to any of them. She already lived with enough heartache, when Jason asked why his friends at the park and in nursery school had fathers and he didn't.

She bitterly recalled the day Jason brought home a flier from school announcing a father-and-son picnic. He wanted to go. She had read the notice, fumed at the injustice, and stormed to the phone to complain about the discriminatory picnic.

The woman stated it was a revered tradition at the private academy, suggesting archly that Liz might elect to keep Jason home that day. Furious, Liz fired off a salvo letting her know what she thought about exclusionary traditions. The day of the picnic, she took Jason to the zoo. Had there had been another neighborhood nursery school she'd have enrolled Jason on the spot.

The following Saturday Jason found his goldfish Ferdie floating atop the water in his bowl. Wearing his Dr. Denton's he'd gone screeching into Liz's room yelling that Ferdie had a new trick. "Come quick!"

She had sat Jason on her lap, explaining to him that Ferdie had died and gone away to a wonderful place, stressing that Jason still had Herman. All Jason wanted to know was when Ferdie was coming back and if the place was so wonderful why couldn't he and Herman go too and how come if Ferdie went away he was floating on top of the water in his fish tank. Liz tried her best to explain life and death, but realized she was failing miserably when Jason began to cry.

The next day she bought another goldfish, which Jason promptly named Ferdie.

Now, to Jason, Joe seemed like the ideal father, promising to play Nintendo games with him, to show him how to throw a football when his leg healed, to take him fishing. As much as she wanted to call the whole summer in Colorado off, she knew she couldn't. What kind of a mother denied her son a summer of pleasure?

"We're here, Joe."

"So we are." He pulled the car to a halt and glanced at her set features, his eyes narrowing. "Liz, I'm sure you've had enough for one day. I know I have. So let's save our argument over the "Daddy" issue for another time. I'll pick you up tomorrow, drop you off at the hospital, then return later on to see Jason. I'm needed on the set."

"No." Liz was determined to clear the air. "Come on into the house. Just for a minute. Please."

Joe shut off the engine, came around to her side to open the door, then walked alongside of her up the stone pathway and into the apartment building, where the doorman greeted her, asking about Jason. After Liz told him he was fine and had no lasting injuries, she and Joe rode up the elevator, immersed in their private thoughts. Joe followed her into the living room.

When they entered, the phone was ringing. Liz dashed over to it, worried it might be the hospital.

Joe flopped onto a chair, throwing his legs on the ottoman, crossing his ankles, and dangling his set of car keys between his fingers.

"Wrong number," she said. Liz took the chair opposite him. On the set, the words were handed to them each day. They could argue, make love, or discuss other people's problems. Regardless of how involved or dramatic the episode, they both knew the outcome of the day's script. Having Joe calmly wait for her to speak unnerved her. Until she opened her mouth she wasn't sure of her first sentence; when it came it was a doozy, lacking in polite preliminaries.

"Joe. How could you allow such a thing to happen?"

"What?" He watched her closely. He hadn't wanted to have this discussion tonight. It would have been better to let time pass, to give her a little perspective. Then he remembered how lost and frightened she'd been, clutching his arm, curling her fingers into his. There was no use trying to dissuade her. She was a mother protecting her cub. He'd have done the same.

"Joe, why didn't you stop Jason? He can't call you Daddy. Can't you see the trouble it's going to cause? My son thinks the sun sets and rises with you. He doesn't know it's a game. Now I'm going to have to be the ogre tomorrow and tell him you were only kidding."

"Don't you dare," Joe said bluntly. "I wasn't kidding him."

"That's even worse," she charged, incensed. "Jason's far too young to know the difference between calling you Daddy for one or two days and calling you Daddy for life. He's a child. A little boy who's desperate for a father so he'll be like the rest of his friends."

"Back up." Joe felt a surge of anger. He dropped his car keys into his jacket pocket. Unbuttoning it, he tossed the jacket on the chair. "In the first place, this is all your fault."

"My fault!"

"Naturally. Who told you to have such a smart son? Most kids his age don't know all about the letter "D." How was I supposed to know where his devious little brain was heading? Apparently you didn't either, because you did nothing to stop him. You're his mother; that's your job. If you think I was going to come on like an ogre to a boy I'd just met, you've got another think coming."

Liz hated to admit that Joe's argument had merit. If she hadn't been intrigued, captivated by Jason's determination, she might have interrupted, nipping this "daddy" absurdity in the bud.

"But what should we do now?" she pressed.

"I'll come up with something that won't be too hard on him."

"We have to do something soon. And what's this 'dear' and 'darling' nonsense?" she asked, envisioning her impish offspring poking Joe's arm. "Don't deny you encouraged him. For your information, we're not dear and darling to each other, we're business associates, Joe, that's all!"

Joe was off his chair, pacing the room, coming back to lean over her, his arms extending on either side of her chair, preventing her from rising. When he spoke, his tone of voice showed his mounting irritation. His blue eyes were intense, reflecting his annoyance. He'd thought today had brought them a lot closer than mere business associates. The term galled him.

"Granted we're merely business associates, Ms. Davis, but you're losing sight of the main point of this discussion. Which you started. You're angry 'cause your son wants to call me Daddy. Well, I've got a flash for you—he surprised the hell out of me too. It's not every day a nice little boy wants to call me Daddy. To be honest, I've got to admit I was touched and flattered by Jason's ingenious ploy. I know as well as you do it's no game to him. But after that heartrending scene did you really expect me to say, 'Sorry, kid, that's reserved for the real McCoy'?" He threw up his hands, knowing he was getting in deeper than he should, yet unable to stop. "Give me credit for some sensitivity, Liz."

He crouched down in front of her, speaking forcefully. "Then I asked myself, Why? Why is a five-year-old boy so desperate to call a man he's known so short a time Daddy? So you tell me why, Mommy? Want to try to hazard a guess?" He spoke with extraordinary forcefulness.

"I have no idea," she fibbed, wishing she'd never brought it up.

"I don't believe you, Ms. Davis," Joe salvoed. "What about the other men you've dated over the years? Did Jason want to call all of them Daddy too?"

"Leave me alone!"

"Try to remember," he prompted, noting the gesture of pride and defiance as she lifted her chin. "Jason's not so old. You can remember back five years, can't you?"

"There's nothing to remember!" she shouted fiercely, resenting his very nearness, his pure male scent, her being with him throughout the day, hearing and seeing other women openly admire him.

She drew on the last embers of her resolve, sorry she had invited him in, wishing he'd leave. If she hadn't been so exhausted, she might have recognized her raw emotion for another emotion. Jealousy. A rotting, gnawing jealousy born of wanting nothing more than to melt against him, to have him hold her, to be with him, not to spend the night alone.

Instead she rose to her feet and turned away from him. She'd said more than she'd intended. "We're talking about Jason."

"No, we're not," he said flatly, dogging her footsteps. "We're talking about Jason's mother." He whirled her around, clamping his hands on her shoulders. "The truth is Jason hasn't met other men. Why haven't you dated? I'm sure men have asked you."

A pulse hammered in her head. "What I do with my private life is none of your business."

"Your son made it my business. Why, Liz?"

"Because I prefer staying home," she said. "Is that okay with you?"

"Why?" he persisted. "Don't try to con me that you don't have any interest in men; I know better."

Abruptly, she raised her head, her cheeks crimson. "For your information, I don't need your pity or your sympathy."

His brow lifted in puzzlement. He rocked back on his heels. "Then?"

"Then nothing," she fumed. She broke his hold, storming past him into the kitchen. "Would you care for coffee? I'm having some."

He positioned himself in her doorway and folded his arms across his chest, observing her. She infuriated him at the same time as she appealed to him. Her flare of anger put color into her cheeks. She sparkled.

"Why?" he demanded.

She slammed the refrigerator shut. "Don't be naive," she said. "The role I play doesn't exactly appeal to men who are interested in being instant fathers."

Joe studied a flustered Liz with an air of shocked realization. "You mean rather than find the good men, you've put yours and Jason's life on hold."

Until now Liz had scrupulously kept her business and private life separate in order to avoid uncomfortable scenes like this. Yet in the short space of time since Jason had been injured she'd had more contact, more sharing, with Joe than she'd ever had with any other man. Jason had never called his own father Daddy, she realized with a pang; only Joe.

"Liz," Joe said softly, "perhaps if we're intelligent we can solve this together. You notice I've dropped the 'dear.' You're perfectly right. We're merely working associates."

Irritation choked her. "Make your point please."

"Just this. It's time for you to resume your social life. Jason would benefit from being around men. Since he already knows me, it's probably not a good idea for me to suddenly drop out of his life." She started to object. "Hear me out first, please. Every time I try to help you, you run like a jackrabbit. Unless you see yourself living alone the rest of your life, you're going to have to change your mind sometime. Now's as good a time as any, especially if the three of us are spending the summer together."

"What are you suggesting?" she asked.

He smiled inwardly. Liz wasn't giving an inch. "All I'm suggesting," he said innocently, "is that we go out on a few dates while Jason's in the hospital. And if you agree, I'll try to get him to call me Uncle Joe instead of Daddy."

"Why?"

"To get to know one another, of course."

"Joe, we already know each other," she said. "We work together every day."

Joe disagreed. He wanted to know Liz much better, and he was preparing to wear down Liz's resolve with the same technique he'd used on his mother when he'd broken four jars of quince-berry preserve at the age of four.

"Not *that* way," he said. "I'm talking about solving the problem of your private life."

"I don't have a problem."

"You only *think* you don't," he said. "I'm looking at this from the perspective of an outsider. Liz, I'm talking real life here. You decided a long time ago men aren't to be trusted."

"Who said I don't trust them?"

"Isn't that what all this is about?"

"Not really. I said most men are interested in the role I play. Those are the ones I'm not interested in." Those and the ones who don't have a stable life. Those who travel and are gone from home so much they forget they took the job for the family, she thought.

"You've got to change your screwed-up way of

thinking; if not, you'll hurt Jason—whom I happen to like, or I wouldn't offer my services."

"Don't do us any favors," Liz replied. She didn't want Joe to ask her out because he felt sorry for her!

An amused smile curled a corner of his lips. "There you go again, leaping to the wrong conclusion. Why can't you accept my offer for what it is? You're probably safer with me than with anyone else."

"Really. Why?"

"I thought that was obvious. You've allowed yourself to get out of the habit of dating, being close to a man. You challenge everything I say as if there's a hidden agenda."

"There is," she said bluntly. "Knowing you, I'd stake my life on it."

"Ridiculous. All right," he said, as if his next words were being dragged from him, "I wasn't going to say this, but you need the reassurance. Lizzy, I kiss you enough during the day at work; you've nothing to worry about on that score. The writers think we're a hot pair. Frankly, and please don't get me wrong, rolling around with you on that hard mattress hurts my knees."

Stunned, she retorted, "That's what you're thinking about while we're kissing! Your damn knees."

"Not entirely," he admitted, enjoying her reaction. No one could look stunned better than Liz. "All that puckering-up of lips and shifting around of our bodies until they've got us so close an envelope couldn't fit between us. And the retakes!" He shook his head sadly, as if he had committed to memory a distasteful task. "The other day when

Shirley Richards was there, it was all I could do not to rub my knees in the middle of our scene. And I know it must be as difficult for you as for me."

She did know. She also wanted to throw the sugar shaker in his fascinating mouth. The bedroom scenes were hard on her for other, more personal reasons. Reasons that sent her to the cold showers with increasing frequency. Joe probably took hot showers to ease the pain in his knees, she thought ruefully.

"Have I said something to upset you?" he asked.

She grinned. "Well, you did mention Shirley Richards," she replied.

"Don't mind her. Let's get back to you," Joe said evenly. "It'll be refreshing for you to share a quiet meal or maybe take in a movie. We can talk about our radio show like business associates do. You'll get back into the swing of things. I'll prove to you all men don't want you to be a siren." He cracked a slow smile.

Liz managed a half smile.

"Do you like to dance?"

"I love to dance."

He raised his brow approvingly. "You do. Then by all means, that's what we'll do."

"Why are you doing this?" Liz demanded, still suspicious. "Do you help little old ladies across the street too?" Was he thinking of her as a basket case while her pulse was tripping so wildly in her throat! she wondered. Then she noticed his previous enthusiastic words contradicted his appreciative perusal, a perusal guaranteed to make Mount Vesuvius erupt.

"I suggest tomorrow night—to take advantage of the hospital's baby-sitting," he said, ignoring her question.

"What about dancing with your bad knees?" she asked.

"They feel fine now."

"You've thought of everything, haven't you?"

"It's my job. You've no idea how lucky you are to have me around, offering myself out of friendship —as long as Jason's in the hospital's expert hands, that is. Call this a goodwill gesture, which I suggest we immediately instigate for Jason's benefit."

At this, Liz's natural good humor returned; a laugh escaped and the coffeepot rattled in her hand. Joe snatched it from her before she burned herself.

She felt giddy, buoyant. "I've never heard a bigger line of bologna in my life. How did we get from fighting to this? We haven't settled a thing. I still don't know how to handle Jason. He insists on calling you Daddy."

"Why don't you let nature take its course, Liz? Things have a way of working out."

"I'm not sure it's wise to let nature take its course."

That's what you think, Liz, Joe thought.

"You say you want your son's happiness. It's time you set about ensuring it." He adopted a clinical air. "I mentioned before that Jason's at an age where he needs a male role model. We can discuss this further tomorrow night. I'd stay, but I'm bushed. I'm ready for bed, aren't you?"

Liz's decision to go on a few dates with Joe had

nothing whatsoever to do with Jason. Had she imagined the quicksilver shift of expression on Joe's face. What was it? Yearning? Desire? Lust? It was gone in the blink of an eye, camouflaged by an air of nonchalance. In any case, she was going to investigate.

On her terms.

Not that she expected to ever fall in love again.

"You really think this is necessary?" It didn't pay to give in too easily, not with Joe.

"Of course," he said magnanimously. "Liz, I'm surprised at you." He was diverted by the beckoning shine on her lips, the sparkle in her eyes. Too bad they weren't on the set now, he thought. Then he'd have a legitimate reason to give her a kiss to knock her socks off. He only hoped he wasn't painting himself into a corner. She didn't know he'd had his eye on her a long time. He'd even extended his contract with *Happy Town* because of her, when he really wanted to go into producing.

"Do you always solve problems this easily, Joe?"

He sent her one of his infuriating grins. "Some solutions take a little longer. 'Night, Lizzy." He closed the door behind him.

Now how, she wondered, does Joe always manage to get the last word? She headed for bed, where she spent the night dreaming about Joe trying to wedge an envelope between their naked bodies.

Had she been able to read his dream she'd have learned it was identical to hers.

•   •   •

Joe's suggestion that Jason call him Uncle Joe worked like a charm, as long as Jason didn't have to be included. Jason's idea of fun was calling Joe "Daddy." Each time Liz pointedly and repeatedly spoke with *Uncle Joe*, Jason would ask *Daddy* to please get him a glass of water, or would order *Daddy* to close the door so that they could be alone. He'd inform Liz that he and *Daddy* needed to discuss men's stuff and would inquire if she could please leave them alone.

Later on in the day Jason's doctor discussed the therapy Jason would require in Colorado. "When the cast comes off he'll need physical therapy for a while to strengthen the calf and thigh muscles. Probably with weights—"

Jason's face lit up. "Weights! Like an athlete, Dad?"

Joe shushed him after telling him yes. Not wishing to create a scene, neither Liz nor Joe corrected the doctor's misunderstanding.

"I was flustered," Liz admitted later that evening at the dinner club. "After all, I didn't want him feeling sorry for Jason. I'll call him tomorrow and set the record straight. He'll understand." And if he doesn't Jason will be out of there in four days anyhow, she thought.

Joe lifted his wine glass. He'd purposely made reservations at an intimate club lounge noted for its good food and six-piece combo. The best part of it was the size of the dimly lit dance floor. If his luck held out, they'd be squeezed together like sardines. "He'll probably recommend a psychologist if you do."

Liz gasped. Had the situation deteriorated so

rapidly? "Do you think so? Jason seemed so happy today."

Joe shrugged. "Naturally. He had me with him. If this keeps up I might have to marry you."

Liz almost spilled her glass of wine. "Don't even joke about that! I'd never marry an actor."

"Oh? Isn't that the pot calling the kettle black?"

"Joe, don't misunderstand me. It's not only actors; it's any man in an occupation where he'd have to travel. I wouldn't do that to Jason. You know how crazy our business is. At any moment a series can be canceled. No, Jason needs stability. I want him going to one school, not a dozen."

"I think you've got your priorities screwed up," Joe said flatly. "Are you planning on quitting acting?"

"I can't. At least not yet."

"Do you want to?"

"As of right now, only if something better comes along."

"Maybe it will," he said vaguely. Liz leaned back in her chair, wondering what he'd meant. She hadn't been sure what he was thinking all evening. He'd showed up on time, given her a quick once-over, then ordered her to get her wrap and purse. For purely selfish feminine reasons, Liz wanted to look her best. She wore a blue sequin strapless gown, zippered up the front, cut high at the thigh. It was designed to show her curves and her good legs. The heels of her black pumps were studded with tiny rhinestones. Joe didn't so much as offer her a compliment. He did, however, pet Herman, who licked his face.

And now Liz was dying to dance. Joe hadn't

made a move to ask her. They exhausted several topics, including books each had read and which movies and actors should win Emmy nods. A couple brushed close to their table, looking adoringly at each other. She looked longingly at the dance floor.

Her toes were tapping under the table. A long, leisurely bath had soothed her. When she was through she'd washed her hair, brushing it until it shone, lifted on one side by a spray of rhinestones.

"Liz, let's dance."

They moved into each other's arms as naturally as if they'd been dancing together for years. As they swayed in time to the music, Liz thought that if the nurses could see Joe in a blue suit, white shirt, and blue tie, they'd envy her. But the least he could have done was tell her her face was clean!

Joe felt his body tighten as it always did when he was near her. He rubbed his lips in her hair, holding her close. She fit against him like a scented glove. His hand slipped up her spine to lightly caress her neck. He spoke with his lips near her forehead. "I was only teasing about the psychologist. Jason's one of the most well-adjusted little boys I know. He'll love Colorado. My folks'll make a fuss over him; he'll play with my niece and nephew. Tom and Frances's children are wonderful. Jason'll fit right in with them, you'll see."

That's what she worried about. Jason would find the family he missed. How would she be able to break him away afterward? Maybe she wouldn't have to . . . She decided to play along with Joe's game.

Joe's hand slipped to the small of her spine. With an imperceptible motion he drew her closer. Liz was scarcely able to speak through the tightness of her chest.

"This is very relaxing," she lied. "Of course, the bubble bath I took before helped."

Joe envisioned Liz luxuriating in perfumed water. His gaze shifted from her face to her glossy hair, her flawless complexion, her sooty-lashed brown eyes. He imagined her in her bath, seeing in his mind's eye her long legs, her rounded hips, her breasts glistening with droplets of oil. He saw her massaging her skin. He saw himself massaging . . .

Liz lifted her eyes to his. They were clear and guielessly blue. Joe was a strong man, with a ruggedly handsome face, reflecting strength of character and humor. A man a woman could spend a lifetime with—provided he stayed in one place.

"Maybe you're right. Five years was a long time to restrict my private life," she said. "I've been selfish, both toward Jason and myself."

Joe nodded, pivoting so the man who'd been staring at Liz from one of the tables, no longer had a good view of Liz.

"Jason's calling you Daddy disturbed me, but then it got me to thinking, especially after our conversation. Children playact continually. But Jason needs to learn there are many forms of families in today's world. Families of affection, not just relation. Nevertheless, I agree with you. I'm about to launch the new, improved me. There's no end of possibilities waiting out there for me."

Joe noticed that several men were openly admiring Liz instead of paying attention to their dates. "Possibilities for what?" Joe asked, blocking her from the view of the worst offender. "Surely you're not intending to jump from abstinence to party animal are you? We don't exactly live in the safest of times."

She snuggled closer. Through the flimsy material of her gown she felt his strong muscular thigh, the texture of his clothes against her silk-clad leg. "Naturally I don't plan on dating *every* night. A leopard doesn't change spots overnight. I fully intend to exercise common sense. You made me realize I'm getting on in years—"

"When did I ever suggest you were getting older?" Joe said, thoroughly annoyed with the turn of events.

She sighed, the sound coming out of her mouth as a purr. "One day I want more children, maybe two," she heard herself admitting. "I'd love a sister and a brother for Jason. With my traditional background, I'm not one who believes in pregnancy without benefit of license."

"Nor should you be," Joe added censoriously.

Liz took heart. "I'm not saying tomorrow, but you have to take credit for being instrumental in all this; that's why I feel it's only right to take you into my confidence."

None of this was making him feel a bit better. "Isn't this a rather sudden turnaround?"

She flicked an imaginary thread from his neck, leaving her hand there. The music was slow and sensual, the lights dimmed to a golden glow. "I weighed your arguments, pro and con. Joe, you can't deny you're the catalyst. There were more pros than cons, especially when I considered Jason's future."

Joe scowled. He hadn't dreamed up this plan for another man's benefit.

"Prudence, Liz. Anyway, you're not going to have time for a while."

"Why not?" She arched her head back, giving him her full attention and a whiff of her perfumed neck.

He stiffled an urge to wring that pretty neck. "You'll be far too restricted this summer."

"Doing what?" She laughed.

"Working with me."

She threw back her head, her full lips parted in a teasing smile, her tiger eyes sparkling impudently. "Then I'll have to wait until fall, won't I?"

Five

The pop of a flashbulb made Liz lift her head. "What was that?"

Joe glanced up, distracted. He was holding Liz closer than he should have been, but she wasn't complaining. He spotted a red-haired young woman in a short-skirted black uniform. "The house photographer's taking a picture at one of the tables. Want one of us for posterity?"

Liz was eager to remain where she was. "Uh-uh; no flashbulbs, no photo opportunities. This is too nice."

He couldn't agree more, although in a way he was sorry. He'd have liked a memento of their first date. Joe contented himself by focusing on her ruby lips. Some of her lipstick had worn off; he wanted desperately to kiss off the rest until they were both breathless. Bewitched, he smiled down at her, finessing her expertly through a tiny opening on the postage-stamp-size dance floor while giving silent approval to its dimensions.

He leaned back and looked at her, a bemused smile on his face. "Are you hungry? The food's getting cold."

Sitting down was the last thing she wanted to do. She shook her head, matching his smile with a dazzling come-hither look. "Not in the least—unless you'd rather take a break." The expensive meal of poached salmon remained untouched on the table.

"You don't hear me arguing," he grinned.

"I could dance all night. It's my favorite pastime. How come I never knew you liked to dance?"

His eyes met hers in a twinkling challenge. "There's a lot about me you don't know."

"I imagine your mother will fill me in on the highlights of your dark past," she teased.

He threw back his head, laughing, then gave her a quick bear hug. "Don't you dare ask her a thing. Mom's apt to spill the beans; then where will I be?"

"Probably in the doghouse again," she said, picturing him as a handsome adolescent. But it was the *man* whose intense gaze caused her to grow emboldened. With the tip of her finger, she pushed away a stray lock of his hair in a familiar manner. Joe bent his head to whisper in her ear. The intimate gestures between them were noted by several people, one in particular.

"Were you that bad?" she asked.

His mouth curved into a grin. "Very. I was an early reprobate, trying my hardest to keep up with my brother. Whatever he did I mimicked. Tonight in your honor, I'm on my best behavior."

Their gazes met, lingered, locked. "Thank you."

You'll never know what this is costing me, he thought.

He enjoyed the physical contact, aware that he knew her as well as any man alive did; yet he didn't know her as well as he wanted. That would come later, in good time, he promised himself. Her skin was soft, intriguing. In the months they'd worked together she'd weaved a magic spell on him, ruining him for other women.

Liz hadn't counted on letting down her guard in public. Because this was new to her, she didn't want to stop. She wanted to rejoice in the security, comfort, and tingling sensation of promise she felt whenever she was in Joe's arms. Happily, she noted the other patrons were interested in their own partners, not in the television stars.

It was years since she'd danced, since she and her ex had frequented some of the hometown clubs during the first year of their marriage. Liz retrieved her meandering thoughts from the past. "Joe, I could dance like this all night."

Gracefully, he pivoted in place, his lips curved in a smile. "On an empty stomach?"

"I'm fine, I assure you."

The rhythm of the music switched to a hilarious bump and grind, reminiscent of the roaring twenties. Joe raised a questioning brow. "Shall we show them how it's done?"

"Lead on, master."

They fell into the spirit, giving a showstopping performance that had the other dancers moving back to give them room. By now, several people recognized the couple from television where they'd first performed this dance. When the music ended, a great round of applause followed. Sweeping in dramatic low bows, they accepted the accolades.

"Not bad." Liz pushed the hair from her face.

"Not bad? Terrific!"

They broke out laughing, pleased with themselves. She laced her arms around his neck as the combo switched to a ballad.

Joe let out a long, quiet sigh of contentment. Liz was more carefree tonight than he'd ever seen her, perhaps as an antidote to all the worry she'd been through.

Liz, who showed the public an image far from the truth, who could adopt a lofty manner, whose cool facade could be called on at a moment's notice. Liz, the temptress of television. Initially it was the public Liz who'd captured his attention; yet it was this private Liz who intrigued him. This was the woman he wanted to make love with. Knowing she was soured by her past experiences, he also knew the television Liz would have made mincemeat of those men, stepping over their bodies without a backward glance. The television Liz never let down her guard. He much preferred the vulnerable Liz who sought shelter in his arms.

Liz sighed blissfully. "Joe, I haven't had such a good time in years. I realize this evening's invitation began as an object lesson, but you outdid yourself. Did you know that until we came onto the floor I was keeping time to the music under the table?"

He sent her a lopsided grin that had her heart

doing flip-flops. "Once or twice you were keeping time on my toes." She laughed.

Before he had realized her intention, she rose on tiptoe to kiss him. It started as a quick, light kiss, but he turned his head, slanting his mouth onto hers, needing to capture her essence. The scent of her raced through him. He needed much more from her; it was a question of how long he'd have to wait.

He traced her lips with his thumb. "I'm glad you're having fun," he said huskily. "That was the general idea."

They danced until the band played its last song. Neither Liz nor Joe took notice of Shirley Richards, who even now was mentally composing this juicy item for the next edition of *Today's Happenings*. The waitress's tip had paid off handsomely. This wasn't a one-shot story.

Tomorrow's column would feature the following teaser:

What glamorous nighttime television star with the initials L.D., and who normally plays a witch, was seen melting in the arms of her handsome costar, whose initials are J.M.? Take it from me, folks, the perky blond is putty in our talented dark-haired hero's hands. It appears these two refuse to stop when the director says, "Cut." This romantic twosome positively sizzles after dark. Stay tuned. I'm sure there's a lot more to follow.

• • • •

Joe waited for Liz to stop yawning. He couldn't suppress a grin. She made a fetching picture standing outside her apartment door in stockinged feet. She sent him an apologetic smile, quickly followed by another yawn. At that he threw back his head, laughing.

"Better go in, sleepyhead. You've got a big day ahead of you tomorrow."

She pouted. She didn't want the night to end. "Don't you want to tell me how I did tonight?" she asked wistfully.

"You were okay, for a beginner," he said.

She leaned into him with a very ungraceful, unladylike thud. "Watch it," she warned, then added, "I was a hit. Did you see that man on the dance floor? The one who wore that garish diamond ring on his pinkie? He never took his eyes off of me."

"Baloney. He was watching the redhead, not you." Joe had seen the man. He'd wanted to punch his lights out all evening.

"I don't want to go to sleep yet," Liz announced, partly due to the pleasant buzz from the champagne, which was making her audacious, and partly to seize the moment before it vanished.

"What do you want?" he asked, tempted to pull the zipper of her dress down.

His mouth was inches from hers. It was more than she could resist. She leaned up against him, drawing his hand to her mouth. Her lips brushed against his palm in a gesture that left him weak.

Her voice was husky as she nuzzled his ear. "I want the whole package. I'd like you to kiss me good night, Joe. Out here in the hall like kids do on Saturday night dates. If anyone catches us, it'll make it all the better—I never did that when I was growing up. Being a policeman's daughter was very restricting, his gun and holster were intimidating. While you were a reprobate, I was Miss Perfect. Kiss me, Joe. Not the way you do on the set. Kiss me like you would if we were high school sweethearts."

What was she trying to do to him? Swallow him by degrees until he couldn't think straight? When he was around her it was as if he'd been waiting for her all his life. On one level, the physical level, they belonged together; they'd proved that in front of millions of people.

He should leap at her offer, but he couldn't be sure whether Liz's request stemmed from a fuzzy head. On the set he was paid to show his emotions; now he struggled to suppress them. He needed much more than a good-night kiss from Liz. He saw in her tiger eyes passion waiting to erupt, even as he was unable to bank his.

He'd been acting with restraint for her sake, yet that was taking its toll on him. If he kissed her he'd want to make love to her; he wouldn't stop until he'd had all of her. And he was afraid that in the morning she'd hate him and herself.

His gaze drifted to her mouth, to her slumberous eyes. "Liz, where've you been lately? High school kids don't just kiss anymore. They're all grown up, with grown-up emotions and birth-control pills. I've held you in my arms all evening; don't ask more of me than I can give. Go to sleep.

Tomorrow you'll thank me. We'll see Jason and everything will be back to normal."

Her heart shriveled in shame. He might just as well have splashed cold water on her. Joe didn't want her! Embarrassment flooded her cheeks. How could she have thrown herself at him, read the signals so wrong? All this time Joe was being Joe, the good-natured, slightly outrageous guy trying to help her get her life back on track.

"The nurses were right," she muttered, rummaging in her purse for her key.

Joe sucked in his breath. He gripped her upper arms, his fingers digging into the flesh. "What the hell are you talking about?"

She flung back her head, tossing her hair past his mouth. How was she going to be able to face him at the hospital tomorrow after making such a fool of herself? Worse! How was she going to be able to go to Colorado? If she had an ounce of brains she'd call the whole thing off.

"Nothing."

Joe lifted her off the floor until they were eye to eye, their breaths mingling. "Nothing, my foot! Look at me, Liz. Right now, there's nothing in the world I'd rather do than kiss you."

She hung onto his shoulders, balancing. "You really don't have to say that; I'm a big girl, remember? I simply forgot my lines. It's entirely my fault."

He slid her down against him, groaning as he felt her breasts pressing against his chest. "The thing is, my sweet little hellcat, that I do want to kiss you. Very much. I happen to like this fantasy of yours. What bona fide date ends with two people shaking hands?" He lowered his head until all she saw was her reflection in his eyes.

"Don't do me any fav—"

Joe silenced her with a kiss that left no doubt in either of their minds that he wasn't fantasizing about mere high school kisses stolen in hallways. She clutched at him when his tongue plunged deeply in her mouth, wave upon wave of feelings ignited by his touch.

She ceased fighting, caught up in a magical whirl, a tangle of desire so encompassing that her heart pumped madly.

Joe was sinking, intoxicated by her wine-rich taste, her utterly feminine scent. He seduced his mind into blankness, letting her weave her powers, promises of nobility damned. He cupped her buttocks, drawing her forward, up high, to his rigid arousal, his lips upon her ears, her eyes, her cheeks.

Liz dragged his lips to hers, growling in his mouth, shuddering for more. Then the sound of the elevator door opening entered their consciousness, and the voices of people entering the hall.

Breathing hard, Joe disengaged himself from her kisses. Her passion had stunned him, enticed him, nearly destroyed him. Liz was reacting to the night; he was reacting to her.

"That's what you asked for, isn't it?" he said without a trace of teasing, looking into her eyes. In them, he read confusion, renewed hurt.

"Liz, for Heaven's sake, this ought to show you I'm no high school youth. Neither am I altruistic. Tonight proved one thing: One of these days you and I are going to make love. When we do, I don't want you waking up the next morning regretting it."

Lightly, his lips touched hers. He kissed her eyes, her cheeks, then gave her another swift, hard kiss. "Think about us, Liz, about why we're waiting; then think about how good it's going to be when you're finally ready."

"But why?" The humiliating question erupted before she could reclaim it. She'd thrown herself at him. He lifted a curl of her hair, and dropped it. Dully, she read the truth, the explanation he omitted, too polite to say.

"Jason?" she mumbled. Joe obviously didn't want her to draw false conclusions.

"It's Jason, isn't it?" she asked, trying to sound casual.

He looked at her in surprise. It took all of his willpower not to touch her. "He's a part of it, Liz."

He saw and accepted the fire in her eyes, the condemnation, even the fury, and then the fierce mother's pride.

Joe took the key from her hand, opened the door, and shoved her gently inside. From somewhere down the hall another apartment door opened and closed. He was unsure if he had the strength to walk down the hall, get in the elevator, and drive home. One thing was certain. He needed a cold shower. Maybe two.

Liz scrubbed chocolate ice cream from Jason's face. After four days in the hospital he was cranky, out of sorts. And so was she. Stan Bernard had called Joe back to shoot some last-minute scenes. Joe's absense, his rejection, his speech, weighed heavily on her mind. He wanted her but he didn't want her. He wanted to make love with her but didn't want her to get any false notions. She couldn't blame him; his life was going along nicely until she'd intruded on it. All she'd been doing these past days was unfairly dumping her problems on Joe; then she'd compounded it by inviting him to mix business with pleasure. And to think that this was supposed to *ease* her way back into the dating game.

Earlier Joe had phoned to say he'd be late. "Jason," she'd said, attempting to soothe her grouchy child. "Joe will be here soon."

"Daddy." He pushed her hand away, turning down his mouth. He was cranky, impatient for his cast to come off so he could walk on his crutches, be independent.

Like her, she thought. The apple doesn't fall far from the tree.

The long hours of confinement in the hospital were getting on her nerves, but she tried hard not to let it show. She drew a chair close to Jason's bed. "Jason, I want you to listen to me, dear. You can't go around calling Joe Daddy. He's not your father, he's a very good friend. Honey, I know you love Joe—he loves you too—but you've got to start calling him by his name. Or Uncle Joe. It's for the best, believe me."

Joe paused in the doorway, frowning. He had overheard her words. In one hand were his newspapers, in the other a game. He rattled his papers to get their attention.

"Hi, you two."

"Daddy! You came," Jason shouted, his face wreathed in a smile. Joe saw Liz's spine straighten. He shrugged his shoulders, as if to say that now wasn't the time to pursue what he'd overheard.

"You brought a basketball game." Jason's voice rose to a happy squeak.

Joe tossed the newspapers on a chair. He began assembling the portable stand and hoop. "No hello?" he asked Liz. Her eyes were big, soft . . . hurt.

"Sorry." She drove her fingers into her palm, her nails biting the flesh. "How was your day? Did anything special happen at work?"

Plenty. On the set, he'd been hit with a copy of *Today's Happenings.* Pictures of him kissing Liz were followed by an article full of innuendos. Everyone had a copy of the paper; one of the crew made the mistake of teasing him, until Joe took him aside to set him straight. "Nothing out of the ordinary."

"I didn't think you were coming," Jason accused.

Joe ruffled the child's hair. "I told you I would, but I was busy at my job. I have to work to make money to pay the bills. That's the way life is, sport. I hope you're being a good boy and not giving your mom a hard time."

"I wasn't," Jason said, a shade too fast.

Joe flipped the ball to Jason, who caught it in his lap. "Liz, why don't you take a break. Maybe bring me a drink or something."

Jason eyed them critically. This was the type of daddy his friends had, the kind who laid down the law, gave out the rules. "I thought you called Mommy dear and she called you darling."

"That was a game, Jason," Joe said gently. "Today I'm calling your mommy by her name, Liz. She calls me Joe; that's my real name."

Jason lost interest in the basketball. "What are you going to call me?" he asked through lowered lids.

"Jason," Joe said. "It's a wonderful name and it suits you perfectly. I bet you didn't know it means *Healer*. It's a much better name for you than Doug."

Jason did not care about the origin of names. He had a one-track mind. "What do you want me to call you?" His lower lip quivered; tears filled his eyes. Joe looked at Liz. She was resplendent in a simple yellow jumpsuit, her hair pulled back in a ponytail. Her eyes looked suspiciously bright too.

Joe sat by the bed, lifting Jason's small hand in his. Why couldn't life be simple, where no child knew pain? The important thing was to get Jason over the hump, out of the hospital, on the mend in Colorado with his family and his brother's family. Whether Liz knew it or not, they could both use a dose of family love.

"How would you like to call me Uncle Joe?"

Jason twisted the edge of his blanket. Blond hair fell over his forehead. He averted his eyes. "Do I have to? I'd rather call you Daddy."

"Even though I'm not your father, Jason?" Joe said gently.

Jason bobbed his head. If he were given a choice he could make a case. "Yes, it feels good. I always

wondered what it would feel like to call someone
Daddy. Now I know. Can I do it for a while, until
we go to Colorado? Then I'll call you Uncle Joe like
the kids there do."

Joe gathered the boy in his arms, feeling the
earnest heartbeat beneath his fingers, the slim
shoulders tucked close to him. Jason lifted his
chin, letting Joe see his earnest face, read the
unsaid plea in his eyes. It was such a small request, Joe thought. One small word was all the
boy asked of him, with a promise to stop. What
that must have cost the youngster! For to Jason,
saying Daddy meant everything. In the corner, Liz
turned her head to keep them from seeing her
cry.

Joe needed a tissue too; the lump in his throat
was unbearable. "Jason," he said, meaning every
word, "you can call me whatever you like." He'd
deal with Liz's objections later.

Jason picked up the basketball. "Good. Okay,
Daddy, let's play. I go first. Mommy, you go get us
a soda like Daddy said." Liz slipped out of the
room. Neither Jason nor Joe seemed to notice her
absence or to know that she silently blessed Joe
for not crushing her son's feelings.

"I tried," Joe said an hour later when they were
in the cafeteria having a cup of coffee while Jason
was napping. In a couple of days Jason would be
coming home, then the three of them would be on
their way West.

"I know you did," Liz assured him. Although
she still wasn't sure how he felt after last night,

it seemed a very casual gesture to reach for his hand.

His fingers curled in response. What would she say if she knew he'd cut the picture of the two of them out of the newspaper, and carefully sealed it in plastic, and that it now rested in his wallet . . .

In his cotton shirt and snug-fitting jeans, Joe looked more handsome than ever.

Everything seemed so complicated today. Her life used to be simple. Work, come home, play with Jason, attend to his needs, read him a story, play the piano, sing with him, shower, climb into bed, write a little on the never-finished manuscripts she wrote as therapy, the ones she relegated to her night table instead of showing her agent. Maybe one of these days, if she got the courage, she'd hand one in, have it critiqued, enlarge her creative sphere.

"Liz, we need to decide what subjects to tackle on our radio show. Our agents have decided the show should be broadcast live."

She was horrified, automatically shaking her head. Maybe Colorado wasn't such a good idea after all. "Absolutely not! We're supposed to interview the guests, right? Where are we supposed to find the talent five days a week in Colorado? We need the luxury of tape. Suppose we flub? What are we going to do?"

"Liz, you know the sponsors have the final word. If they prefer it live we'll do it live from my house. They've hired a fine technician, Pete Keeting, to help us. There's no reason we can't have guests flown out to Colorado.

"I've brought along some radio tapes of some old shows for inspiration. Tonight, take them home and listen to them; you'll see you've got nothing to worry about. Call-in questions from the listening audience will be featured too."

"Suppose one of them asks an improper question?"

"We're using a thirty-second delay to screen out the crazies. The more I think about this the more I'm glad you talked me into it."

She looked at him. It was true; the more he became involved in the preparation, the more he liked the idea of this radio show. Everything was getting away from her. Jason. The show. Colorado. *Joe;* it all came back to him.

"Joe, if you spend all of your time on the show, how are you going to help your father in the store?"

"By making him hire more help. Between my mom and me we'll cover the bases. I'll still have plenty of time to devote to us. Dad has a fine store manager now."

Joe's gaze flicked briefly to her mouth, thinking of another way to allay her fears. But not now. "The network's scheduled us for a time slot of five to five-thirty P.M. It gives us plenty of time. There's an extra car which you can use to bring Jason to the hospital for therapy. You and I can read the newspapers over breakfast and decide on future topics. We're free on the weekends; if you like, we can all go sight-seeing."

"Okay," she said. She looked up and felt it again. That kindling of flame whenever Joe was near. There's nothing Joe Michaels can't do, no problem he can't solve, she thought. She'd seen him in operation on and off the set.

His voice interrupted her thoughts.

"Liz, this will work; we'll make it work. You and I are pros, there's nothing we can't do. I've given it plenty of thought. There's a lot of local talent who'd jump at the chance to be interviewed on radio. Think of all the authors who want to tout a book. Restaurant chefs. Politicians—"

She scoffed at that. "Why would a New Yorker care what goes on in Colorado? If the show isn't about skiing in Aspen, I doubt if there's a national audience." Liz morosely cupped her face in her hands. Why had she let Joe talk her into going to Colorado?

"Perhaps not," he argued, amused, having witnessed the same dour expression on Jason's face a few minutes ago. "There's always celebrities in Aspen who'd be willing to be interviewed."

She raised her eyes, unable to hide her concerns. "Joe, be practical. What's the talent budget?"

"Not that much," he admitted, avoiding telling her the budget was meager. They were expected to draw on their knowledge of theater and topical events.

Since the budget was so low, Joe was certain the gossip item had actually been a blessing in disguise. A little free publicity—and a way of letting other celebrities know that being connected with Liz and Joe would give them exposure.

But he knew Liz wouldn't agree. Joe decided to wait until they were in Colorado to tell her about the Shirley item. And that Shirley had agreed to be their first guest. Why upset her now?

"Where's your spirit of adventure?" he asked, setting her cup in front of her. "May I remind you this was your idea in the first place? I just went along for the ride. I'm looking forward to debating the issues with you, knowing how you adore arguing."

"I do not!"

"See, you're starting already."

Amused and exasperated, she said, "Suppose I agree with you?"

"Then we throw the topic out or you pretend." He discovered he liked talking to Liz about the show. It was entirely their own to nurse through its infancy. He really enjoyed being able to work on the preparation and the production aspects.

Darkness was falling. Joe gave Liz a long, silent appraisal. He'd kept her out late last night, and she looked like she needed some rest. He glanced at his watch. "Isn't it time we leave?"

"In a little while. I want to stay with Jason a bit longer. Joe, I must have been out of my mind, agreeing to do a radio show, then talking you into it too. Here I am about to move my injured son, fly out to a state I've never seen, intrude on your parents, whom I don't know, and upset their routine by using your home for business. It's insane. I shouldn't be doing this."

"That's ludicrous. I want you to listen to me, and listen good. The only thing you should be worrying about is finding a temporary home for Herman and Ferdie. Leave the rest up to me."

She half-rose with a start. "Goodness! I forgot all about them . . . I'm still not sure."

Joe encircled her wrist. "Do you want to go

upstairs, tell Jason he's not going trout-fishing with me? Not going to meet Tom and Frances's children, one of whom is close to his own age? Not have fun in my dad's toy store? Not have me teach him football when he's better? Not play Nintendo games? If you do, you're going up alone. I refuse to be a party to it . . . You know, I've never known you to have cold feet where work is concerned."

"It's more than work," she said. "It's everything. Like last night."

Joe drew back a moment. "Ah, so that's it. Recriminations already. The dinner, the dancing, or what came later?"

"What came later. The kiss."

"Was it that bad?" he asked gently. For him it had been wonderful. With no cast and crew watching, they'd shared their first kiss in private.

Liz nearly lied. Until now she'd protected herself and her son from unnecessary problems by keeping their lives on a steady, even keel. If she were perfectly honest sometimes the calmness bored her. Nothing about Joe was boring. His steady gaze prevented her from lying. Her breathing was unsteady, her voice low. "You know it wasn't; it was wonderful."

"Then what?" he pressed, wishing they were alone.

"We're going to be cooped up in the same house."

Even as his body responded to the suggestion that they'd be sharing the same roof, he knew he'd never take advantage of her. He was annoyed she'd think so little of him. "Liz, we're grown people, in control. Last night proved we're human. Don't forget, we've been thrown together in unusual circumstances."

Liz shifted to ease the pain in her back. Whenever she was tense, the pain reminded her she needed to relax. Joe saw it.

"Your back?"

"Uh-huh."

He rose. "Come on, I'm taking you home."

"I've got to stay with Jason."

"We'll go upstairs now, kiss him good night, and leave. It's not as though he has a life-threatening illness. Liz, you've got a life too. It's about time you start attending to your needs."

Six

Liz's invitation came between "Welcome to our show" and "We'll be right back after a word from our sponsors."

Joe spit out the olive in his mouth. He was glad this was a private rehearsal at her house.

Seated yoga-style on the floor, Liz wore pink clam diggers, a long-sleeved, bright green T-shirt that had seen better days, and nothing on her feet. Joe wore a gunmetal-gray sweat suit. He had removed his sneakers an hour ago. The oozing remnants of a pepperoni and sausage pizza gelled in its cardboard box on a footstool. Opting for the carpeted floor, their backs were propped against the sofa, old radio scripts in their laps.

"Come again?" he said at length.

She'd been holding her breath, protecting herself against disappointment, her stomach tied in knots, her hands clammy.

She cleared her throat. Just think of this as

one of our scripts, she told herself. "I said I think we should get the sex out of the way."

It was a while before he found his voice. When he did, he didn't sound enthusiastic.

"That's what I thought you said."

"So," she said, her tone as bland as if she were inquiring whether he wanted to go ice-skating. "What do you think?"

For a moment he drifted, caught up in a daydream, envisioning her invitation. Then the moment passed, replaced by a slow-burning resentment.

Not trusting himself, he took a long, slow swig of beer. She was doing it to him again, pushing his buttons. What right did Liz have to sit next to him on the floor, her brown eyes calmly fixed on him, awaiting a response to her proposition.

In his version of this *scene*, it wouldn't be a let's-get-it-over-with chore. He'd pour vintage wine from a crystal decanter, she'd lay amidst a carpet of rose petals strewn on black satin sheets, Rigaud vanilla candles would frame the bed, and a faint breeze would billow the curtains.

He twiddled the beer bottle between his thumb and forefinger, sloshing the brew.

"You're sure this is what you want?" His tone approached boredom.

Liz had given their situation a lot of thought. It wasn't an arbitrary decision to ask him to go to bed with her. She'd never thought of herself as a woman vulnerable to infatuation, but if this wasn't infatuation it was something far worse, far more dangerous to her well-ordered existence, the road she set for herself and Jason.

Between one and two A.M. she'd stopped tossing and turning. She had rights too! Up until now most of the suggestions had been Joe's. All she'd done was act on them. Well this time she'd make the proposition.

Once. Then she could get on with her life.

She hadn't wanted to seduce him! Playing the seductress was too much like her television character. Besides, in real life seduction didn't come naturally, not when she was so nervous.

"It's now or never," she said, struggling to maintain her composure.

Joe wanted to throttle her. When he was with her something happened. His palms sweated, his heart beat a little faster. He felt like a man in distress.

"Sort of like a command performance?"

She shrugged and lowered her eyes.

Joe looked dubious. "This isn't quite the way I figured it would happen. I may be an actor, but I'm not a performing seal."

She gulped. She glanced down at her hands, then back at him. She moistened her lips. "It's the best I can do on short notice. The chances are it won't mean anything, and then we can go on the way things were, without wondering."

He leaned back, his face thoughtful. "Without wondering the whole time we're in Colorado, you mean. Is that it?"

"It crossed my mind," she admitted.

He snorted. "Very practical."

"I was hoping you'd see it that way. We don't

want this interfering with our work, do we? It could; don't you think so?"

He finished his beer, wiped his hands, and rose. "Then I guess we'd better get at it."

She had planned to change into an alluring nightgown, fix her face, style her hair, put on perfume. "Now?"

His laugh was pure male. "Wasn't that the general idea?"

She put on a brave face. "Aren't you going to help me up?"

He looked shocked. "And spoil the romantic moment, Liz? Hell, I figured you've got this seduction scene all worked out in your mind. As they say, lead on—unless you'd rather do it on the floor near the pizza box."

"The bedroom will be fine," she stammered.

His lips tightened. "Well, come on then. Perhaps with a little encouragement on your part I'll be able to do mine." There was a hard, cold edge of steel to his voice.

She hadn't counted on his anger. Surprise, yes. Maybe even a little laughter, some teasing to ease the situation; but not his icy, withering look. She recoiled from it. Hadn't he said he wanted to make love with her when she was ready?

"You're angry."

"Me?" His eyebrows rose, his tone cruelly mocking. "Why should I be angry? Now's as good a time as any." His gesture encompassed the room. "We've eaten, we've gone over the script, Herman's napping, Ferdie's swimming in his bowl, you don't have to worry about Jason since he's safely in the hospital. It's just us, baby. I'd say you thought of everything. Do we shower first or does that come later, or do you usually skip that part? I want to get this right on the first take."

Her eyes smarted. She was forced to raise her head to see his face. "You're hateful." She scrambled up, bumping his thigh. "Forget it."

He reached for her then, swinging her hard against him. With lightning speed his lips and hands were everywhere, shedding her clothes while at the same time carrying her into the bedroom. He threw her roughly onto the white bedspread.

Before Liz knew what was happening, Joe had stripped out of his clothes and was looming like an angry lion before her. "I imagine you had this bedroom farce all worked out, didn't you? Tell me, Liz, was I supposed to be grateful over your invitation to taste your tender body, morsel by morsel, the way you have me grovel on television? Let me know, baby; I don't want to overstep my bounds."

He came to her then, pulling her into his arms, covering her body with his, matching his anger with the punishing kisses he rained on her body, her face, her lips.

She began to struggle, pushing ineffectually against his chest. Liz couldn't smell anything but his male aroma, feel anything but the arms locking her in a vise. "I thought you wanted me, the other night—"

He found her lips, snatching away her words with his marauding mouth while his hands massaged her leg and kneaded the inside of her thigh. He caressed her breasts, then covered them with his mouth, sucking first one nipple, then the other, until she cried out against her will in passion. He murmured his satisfaction as her hands delved into his hair. He lifted his head, his eyes a furious azure.

"The other night I was talking about making love, not performing like a studhorse, but if that's what you want that's what you'll get."

"No!"

Liz's only coherent thought was to put an end to the mockery she'd begun. Despite his anger, his kisses gentled, his hands made her come alive, but this wasn't the way she wanted it either. No amount of acting could hold back the tears that fell on his arm.

With a savage snarl he flung himself away, laying back on the pillow, his arm across his eyes. The only sound in the room was the sound of their heavy breathing. He was in love with her, deeply, irrevocably in love. And she'd made it impossible to tell her. He heard her cry, and when her hand slipped into his, he knew he was lost. He sat up.

She shuddered, her hand tentatively touching his spine.

"Joe, don't leave, not this way. I don't know what it is when I'm with you. You excite me, I feel right with you—"

"Careful, Liz. You might start to say something you'll be sorry for." He didn't want to hear her reply. She rolled toward him, kissing his chest.

It was over as suddenly as it had begun, the anger he felt, the fury at her for not recognizing what they could have together. Her plea served to ignite the flames, kindling his voracious need for her.

"Liz, do me a favor. The next time you invite me into your bed, let me write the lines. Yours stink."

"What would you have written, Joe?"

Desire made him dangerous. And edgy. "You're afraid to come to Colorado unless the sex is out of the way first, isn't that right?"

"Partly." She shook her head. "Yes, I guess that's right."

"Why?"

"Before you came into my life I knew what I wanted. Then you made me question everything. I was furious at first, then annoyed. Jason and I lived a nice, quiet life with Herman, Ferdie, and Fiona. My life is exactly opposite to the one I portray on television. It's how I feel comfortable."

He nodded without interrupting.

"After Jason's accident you became a part of our lives. You were kind and caring. When we danced I felt carefree. Later I practically threw myself at you. You said that you wanted me, that one day we'd make love. Your only requirement was that I wouldn't wake up in the morning with regrets. I have no regrets, Joe."

She let out a careful breath.

Joe lay down, leaning on his elbow, his hand resting on her hip. He wanted her desperately, more each day. Spending the hours, the kind of time they'd had together only added to his need for her. He knew her fears of trusting another man with her heart, her fears that he'd travel off into the wide blue yonder, leaving her and Jason. Yet here she was offering herself to him.

"It's amazing how being in love doesn't enter into it. Just a case of nerves, huh? That sure as hell isn't the most romantic proposal I've ever received—understandable perhaps, but not romantic."

"Joe, love and romance have been out of my life a long time, but that doesn't mean I don't have feelings too."

"No one can fault you for that." Abruptly, he rose from the bed and pulled her off unceremoniously.

"What are you doing?" she asked, placing her left foot down for balance.

He grabbed her wrist. "Liz, not only do you write lousy opening lines, but there are times you shouldn't be asking questions."

He stopped long enough to kiss her open mouth as she started to protest, then dropped another kiss on her naked breast.

"Please, Joe, I hate surprises."

"You're gonna love this one."

He lifted her boldly in his arms, carried her into the shower, turned on the jets, and began to make love to her. There wasn't an inch of her body he left unloved as his hands soaped and caressed her.

When his lips showed her he meant it when he said he wanted to taste all of her, she lost control, clinging to him, clutching his shoulders, gasping with the thrill of it, of him, no longer caring whether they were on a bed, a beach, the floor, or beneath a waterfall. His tongue ignited her, causing her to arch her hips as he lifted her legs around him, plunging into her.

As far back as she could remember she'd wanted to belong, to share. With him she'd been granted her wish. Taking him deeper, she kissed him fervently. His lips were upon her throat, dissolving all her thoughts with an urgency to give what he gave, making the kind of love to her she'd only imagined in her wildest dreams. The throaty cries in the steamy shower could have come from him or her.

He carried her back into the bedroom, reverently toweling off the dampness. She had wanted him, just as he wanted her. She wanted to touch him, to have him touch her, to possess his body as he possessed hers. As he kissed her she felt her body coming to life, seeking the fulfillment only Joe could give. Softly her hands caressed him, matching his actions.

He treated her like a precious jewel, a priceless wonder, praising her, her beauty, how she made him feel. Joe was aggressively male. He made her quiver, tingle in anticipation, bringing her time and time again close to that peak until she thought she would go mad. When it happened, when she teetered on the edge of flight, then soared free, he was there to join her.

"Why the shower, Joe?" she murmured later, her fingers busy with a curl of chest hair.

He dropped a languid kiss on her belly.

"No writer ever wrote that scene for us," he said simply.

A warmth of feeling rushed through her, then she turned in his arms, bringing his mouth to hers. "No writer could."

"Mmmmm, don't stop," he said as she began to explore his body again.

He had a marvelous, strong body, she thought

possessively. She ran her toes up his thigh. He had muscles everywhere. She'd felt them grip her in passion, hold her while the storm receded. His waist was trim, his torso firm.

A disciplined body.

An actor's body, she reminded herself. A man who could be away for months, working on another continent at a moment's notice. He'd said he might leave *Happy Town*.

Sighing, she turned her head, her hair was wild, mussed from his hands. "Joe, this presents a problem for us, you know." Their lovemaking, which began as a frantic coupling, had eased into a delicious, exploratory session.

"What kind of problem?" He lazily stroked her spine.

"How are we going to keep our hands off each other in Colorado? I refuse to dishonor your parents' home."

"Spoken like a true cop's daughter; however, I agree with you. We'll work something out. There's no way I'm going to keep my hands off you now."

Even with the intimacy they'd shared, they were still two independent people who needed to learn a lot more about each other. And there was Jason.

"Joe, we can't get serious."

He kissed her forehead. "Too late. I'd say we've already gotten pretty serious." His tone was soft, but his words let her know that nothing, since they'd entered that shower, could ever be the same again. But he knew she'd deny what she was really feeling. So rather than argue, he began to distract her, mercilessly using whatever delights he had in his arsenal. For Liz, the whirlwind began again. She closed her eyes as waves of sensations caught her up in a tide.

"Relax, Lizzy. You worry too much." He dipped his head, licking her skin in a sensitive spot. He found her secret place, laughed in satisfaction as her eyelids grew heavy. He brought her hand to him.

"Joe," she moaned, dragging him up to her.

"Careful, you might get serious." But she didn't reply. His hand was doing that, so she started doing this, the two of them getting their cues all wrong as they tossed out the script, immersed in rediscovering each other.

If she'd wanted to, she could have fooled herself into thinking they were a family. After working on plans for the radio show, he arrived at the hospital with a kiss for both Liz and Jason, plus a present for the boy. It didn't matter to Jason whether it was an expensive toy or a rock with interesting formations, as long as it was an object shared by all.

Jason mended well; there was no leg swelling. He'd quickly become a favorite of the nurses, showing them simple card tricks he'd learned from Joe. But he wanted out and made no bones about it. "I miss Herman and Ferdie," he moped, but his glum look turned to one of joy when Liz told him he'd be going home in two days.

He'd been measured for a cast. His physician had made a courtesy phone call to Joe's brother, Tom, who would be in charge of his care in Colorado.

Liz set aside her concern about the growing bond of love between Jason and Joe. How could she blame her son for loving a man she loved too? She refused to examine this feeling of oneness with him. Instead she defined it as an "affair," which in her mind was easier to deal with, since it didn't involve a future.

Love wasn't mentioned between them. Once or twice Joe attempted to bring up the future, but she immediately changed the subject. "Let's not spoil everything. Let's enjoy the summer."

Joe would give her a hard, penetrating look, then shrug his shoulders.

He didn't hide his feelings for the boy, nor did Jason hide his for Joe. They got along so well that when Joe corrected Jason's behavior at times, Jason happily chirped, "Sorry, Dad."

"Joe, he's got to start calling you Uncle Joe."

"He will," Joe said equably. But he didn't.

Joe read to Jason while Jason ate dinner. When the youngster finished he read his beginner books to Joe with surprising ease, basking under the praise Joe heaped on him.

Liz cautioned, "Joe, it's going too far."

She was combing her hair at the time. He'd been watching her, seated in a chair. He threw up his hands, a study in disgust. "Since when is love going too far? Have you decided to ration the amount of love you'll allow your son?" Ashamed, she couldn't argue when she herself clung to Joe for the same reason.

Though she hadn't been on the set since Jason's accident, Liz accepted an invitation to the *Happy Town* wrap party. Liz loved being back among her fellow actors, exchanging gossip. No one mentioned the glow in her eyes when she looked at Joe or the heated gaze when his eyes found hers.

Many had privately teased him the day after Shirley Richard's piece on them was printed. But knowing Liz's penchant for privacy, he warned them to keep quiet. No one mentioned the story to Liz.

On their last evening Liz and Joe explored the city, prowling the East 70s, darting into antique stores to browse.

At one store Liz made a purchase. "Did you need to buy that ugly thing?" Joe asked when they were back on the street. He stroked the belly of a red-painted, laughing figurine with a garish gold belly button, its wooden arms outstretched.

She slipped her arm through his. "Of course not."

"Then why did you buy it?"

She poked his ribs. "It's for you, silly. He reminds me of you."

"How?"

She giggled. "Joe, you don't get to see what I see." She ran her fingers down his flat stomach.

"You see the best sights," he teased. "Too bad the ones I see are so boring."

He pulled a squealing Liz into his arms. His eyes seemed as dark as midnight, his arms a welcome vise. "How do you like that?"

"I love it." She threw her arms around him, giving as good as she got. No one bothered to look as they exchanged a deeply satisfying embrace. No one cared.

Like tourists, they strolled arm in arm along the colorful streets of Greenwich Village, finding neighborhood haunts. They ate to their hearts' content, telling each other they'd work it off later—with their own special exercise regime.

Which they did.

To help launch the talk show, the radio station in Colorado had put out publicity, capitalizing on the popularity of the soap and its stars. The wire services carried the news too. Additionally, Joe placed phone calls to friends whom he knew were flying to the Coast, asking them to schedule a stopover in Colorado to guest on their show. All were enthusiastic to learn the program was going to be aired coast-to-coast.

"Amazing what a little arm-twisting does," he joked to Liz.

"Leaving so soon?" she murmured. She was still glowing from the night of love in Joe's arms.

Joe gathered up his shaving gear and stowed it in its case. He was still amazed at how much she meant to him. If it were possible for time to stand still he'd want it to be now, with her champagne-blond hair spilling on the pillow, her skin dewy from lovemaking, her eyes saying she was sorry he was leaving.

If only, he thought, the time were right for him to make a declaration. But Liz seemed content to let matters drift along. She'd already told him that if she ever remarried it wouldn't be to a man whose profession could take him away on a moment's notice. Unfortunately, his present business offered no such guarantees.

And Jason still called him Daddy.

Liz viewed what had happened between them as a culmination.

He wanted a beginning.

Returning to the bed, he leaned down to nuzzle her neck. "Do you have a better idea?"

She gave him a steamy look. "I thought you hated my ideas."

"Not all of them. In fact, I like some of them a lot." He slipped his hand beneath the sheets.

"Joe!" she gasped, squirming away.

The shaving kit fell to the floor. It was a long time before he bothered to pick it up.

Seven

Jason hunkered down on his crutches, his right leg encased in a fiberglass cast inscribed with so many doctors' and nurses' names in brilliant Day-Glo colors that he could have passed for a fluorescent medical advertisement.

Joe and Liz had arranged for his release to be a festive affair, complete with balloons and gifts for everyone who'd been involved in Jason's care. Jason soaked up the attention, until the nurses started to plant kisses on his cheeks.

"I want to go home," he announced. "I want to see Herman and Ferdie."

Liz was dressed in a creamy yellow Givenchy suit, a plum silk blouse, and black pumps. Her skin glowed, because Joe had given her a massage the night before.

Once Jason was safely back inside his home, the air in her house turned hectic. Liz wished she hadn't made her travel plans for the same day as Jason's release from the hospital. Joe seemed calm. He lounged by the door, eyeing a frenzied Liz darting back and forth, stuffing luggage with last-minute items.

"Liz." Joe tapped the face of his watch. "I'd like to take off before the plane does."

She absentmindedly drummed three fingers on her mouth.

"I know I'm forgetting something."

'Liz, there are stores in Colorado Springs. You're packing everything you own."

She half-turned. "I hate buying the same thing twice. Besides, most of this is Jason's."

Jason maneuvered over to his mother. "Mommy, why can't Herman and Ferdie come too?"

"They don't like to fly."

"They never tried it."

"Please, Jason."

"Well they haven't," Jason persisted.

Liz's nerves snapped. "Jason! Herman and Ferdie stay. That's it."

Joe stepped over to Jason, speaking quietly, ushering the youngster toward the door.

Jason craned his neck, listening attentively. When Joe finished, he bobbed his head.

"Okay, Mom. Herman and Ferdie stay. They're afraid of heights anyhow."

Liz sent a glance of appreciation in Joe's direction. "I'm sure I've forgotten something." She walked back into the bedroom for a lightweight jacket.

"Liz, we're going to my parents' house, not to the wilds of Africa."

His home, not hers, she thought. *Everything would change between them.*

Although she was nervous about her relationship with Joe, she no longer had trepidations about doing the show live. Joe had taken care of that with their practice sessions. If the actual broadcasts came off as well, they'd have a quality product. Her real problem was her increasing need for Joe. She simply couldn't accept the thought of a mate whose job description included following the sun if necessary to work. Long ago she had made a vow not to leave Jason, to give him a sense of continuity, of belonging to a community. He was school-age now, and she owed him that much.

Not that Joe had broached the subject of marriage. He talked of her future in general terms, of Jason's in specific terms—of the boy's need for male role models, for a constant love. He did not talk of "Liz and Joe." She remembered, not happily, that he'd told her he had led an active social life.

The tables had turned. While she considered dropping the radio project, Joe's enthusiasm for the new adventure continued to grow. He seemed more and more enthralled with the workings behind the scenes, and the marketing of the show.

"It's only sensible to explore this medium," he told her. "We'll get the five o'clock rush-hour traffic; that's a big audience. There's no telling where this can lead."

The truth was that Joe had other motives for keeping Liz interested in continuing the program. He discovered that his creative juices flowed with ideas for packaging shows.

But Liz showed signs of being intimidated with the entire trip. The phone call that morning from his parents seemed to be the catalyst. When she spoke now of his mother's kindness in welcoming her and Jason long distance, Joe detected a note of strain. "She's being tremendously kind," she said.

Joe leaned back on the couch. "Then what's wrong?"

"Your mother said they're meeting us at the airport."

He took both of her hands in his. "That's not unusual—we need a ride home. Mom and Dad always meet me when I come home."

"Six of them," Liz wailed. She felt awful for her unappreciative attitude. "Tom, Francis, Janice, and Mike are coming too. It's a cast of thousands."

She swayed toward him, to the comfort and security of his embrace. She'd have much preferred to arrive without fanfare instead of being given the once-over en masse, being dropped into the circle of Joe's close-knit group. She'd be the odd woman out—a stranger with a child. And once thing perplexed her: His mother had mentioned to her seeing their picture in the local paper; but before Liz could ask her about it, Joe had taken the receiver.

"I think this all might be too much for Jason," she told him.

You mean it'll be too much for you, Joe thought to himself.

"Honey, after seeing Jason's exit from the hospital, I'd say your son can handle a large audience. Quit worrying, Liz. Besides, it's not really six. My brother has his own car. He'll go back to his own house from the airport. Don't forget," he added gently, "we haven't seen each other in a long time."

But Liz couldn't shake off the feeling that she missed a link of crucial information.

Liz heard Fiona's lilting brogue from the other room, attempting to coax Herman out from behind the sofa. Taking refuge in familiar haunts, the poodle acted as if it knew a momentous change was about to occur.

Liz handed Joe her blue leather makeup case, continuing with her train of thought. "Joe, your mother said she saw a picture of us in the paper. I don't recall any recent publicity shots, do you?"

Joe disregarded the question by saying he needed to help Fiona with Herman. Damn. Her query couldn't have come at a more inopportune time. Liz would really feel uncomfortable if she knew his parents had seen the intimate picture of them at the nightclub. And on top of that, he still had to break the news that his agent had arranged for Shirley Richards to be their first guest. Everything seemed to be out of his control.

From his mother's hints and her encouraging tone of voice, he suspected she'd already concluded that he was bringing his future wife home to meet the folks. If his suspicions were correct, he didn't dare tell Liz, not even for a laugh. He knew she'd refuse to board the airplane.

"Liz," he said, depositing the wriggling Herman into Fiona's arms, "We have to go—the limo's here."

Liz looked up and saw the driver at the door. With a nod from Joe he lifted two suitcases, saying he'd be back for the rest.

"I'll write and call you often, Fiona," Liz promised. "Thanks for taking in Herman and Ferdie. We'll be back before you know it."

"Take good care of them, Joe."

Liz gazed out the window at the sapphire-blue sky, mesmerized by the clouds whipping past her window.

The stewardess handed her a glass of orange juice. "Jason's fallen asleep, Ms. Davis. Shall I throw a blanket over him?"

Smiling, Liz glanced across the aisle at Joe and Jason. The boy rested on Joe, their hands intertwined over Jason's stomach. His right leg was sprawled outward at a comfortable angle. Both were sound asleep. "It looks as if the two of them could use one. Do you mind?"

The stewardess smiled. "It's not every day I get to meet two television stars. He's gorgeous, isn't he?"

"Mmmmm," Joe in repose resembled a child: innocent, trusting, guileless. Liz sipped her juice, memories flooding her mind. Joe awake was something else: formidable, strong, loving, argumentative, humorous.

All the qualities she wished for in a man.

She'd thought about their blossoming relationship a hundred times, telling herself not to read too much into it.

Joe made her fantasies come true.

He was easy to love, too easy. He was the perfect, charming companion. She didn't even mind his temper; in fact, she enjoyed sparking it. Joe was the man for her—but only to date, not to marry. He lacked the essential ingredient: geographical stability.

"We'll be landing soon," the stewardess said.

Joe stretched, yawned, then glanced down at Jason, who shifted in his seat as he came awake. "We're landing, Jason." He brought Jason's seat to an upright position, securing the seat belt.

Jason cocked his head. "I like flying. You know something, I bet Herman and Ferdie would too."

"I bet you're right, son."

Jason beamed.

They waited for the other passengers to deplane before taking Jason out. The airline had a wheelchair waiting on the jet ramp, but the boy balked. "I'm using my cruthces."

When the three finally made it to the lounge, they heard a shout, "There he is!" Six-year-old Mike was the first to spot his famous uncle. A flurry of hands bobbed up and down, waving to Joe, Liz, and Jason.

What followed was bedlam, with all the members of Joe's family pumping hands, hugging, kissing, asking a million questions at once. Liz and Jason stood quietly outside the circle until Joe finally extracted himself. Jason stood quietly, enthralled by the whole experience.

As promised, the entourage consisted of Edna and Vernon Michaels, Joe's parents, and his brother Tom, his wife Frances, and their two children, Mike and Janice. Janice was eight, she proudly told Jason.

Liz was embraced in a bear hug by Joe's brother Tom. Tom was tall, clean-cut, and sported a red mane. He had bottle-green eyes that danced merrily. She was reminded of the stories Joe told about his brother's mischievous childhood.

"I don't believe in waiting for this big lug to introduce us. Welcome to the Springs, Liz."

Then he bent down, giving a professional appraisal of Jason's leg. "I'm especially glad to meet you, Jason. You're doing very well on those crutches."

"I'm next." Frances elbowed her way into the little group.

Liz smiled at Joe's sister-in-law. She and Tom made quite a pair. She was as dainty and petite as he was tall and broad. "We'll talk later, when you're not so overwhelmed by a gaggle of Michaels," Frances said. Liz liked her immediately.

"And these are my parents, Liz," Joe said proudly.

Edna Michaels had red hair, green eyes, was of medium height, and was possessed of a lively wit and a sharp eye. She saw the possessive look in Joe's eye and smiled to herself. "Welcome to our family, Liz. I hope Colorado Springs agrees with you."

Vernon pumped her hand. Almost six-feet, he leaned debonairly on a cane. His face was leaner than his son's; there was an elegance, a grace to this man whose love of the west had brought him to Colorado. "You're a mighty pretty young woman. From watching you on television, mighty talented too. And you must be Jason. How're you managing on those crutches?"

"Fine," Jason replied.

The older man and Jason began to speak about

their respective disabilities. Edna interrupted, handing Jason a package. "This is especially for you."

As the youngster thanked Joe's mother, Vernon added, "If you like, young man, I'll show you the store. Something tells me there's another present waiting for you on one of the shelves."

Liz felt a lump in her throat. Nothing could have made Jason feel more included in the family group.

"Why don't I come out to the house in a few days and take Jason home with us for the day?" said Frances. "He and Mike seem to have hit it off—at least they haven't killed each other yet. My theory is Mike's jealous of the crutches." Frances held her daughter's hand.

"I'd be very grateful," Liz replied, "Joe and I have so many things to do before next week, when the program airs."

"A long time ago my mother taught me it's not polite to stare," Vernon said to Liz, "but I know she'll forgive me this one time. Joe, you're a mighty fortunate man to work with this young lady."

"She's lucky to work with me, you mean," Joe joked.

Edna said, "The picture in the paper doesn't do you justice. You're a lot prettier in real life—isn't she, Joe?"

"What picture?" Liz asked.

"Let's go." Joe took her elbow, guiding her toward the carousel, where the luggage was coming onto the ramp.

"The picture of you two smooching," Mike said.

Janice puffed out her upper lip and cuffed her

brother on the back. "It's not smooching, bird-brain, it's kissing." She turned to Liz. "He means the one where you and Uncle Joe are kissing at the nightclub. Grandma said we weren't supposed to mention it."

"What's such a big deal about that?" Jason piped. "I see Daddy kissing Mommy all the time. Isn't that right, Mommy?"

Eight

Explanations for Jason's bombshell use of the
term "Daddy" were mercifully put on hold as everyone suddenly remembered vital bits of news to
impart to Joe, who didn't seem at all shocked at
being called Daddy. Smiling at his "son," he bent
down to answer one of Jason's questions.

Keep smiling! Liz told herself. Things couldn't
get any more embarrassing. She'd deal with the
two of them later.

Nevertheless, she enjoyed the drive to the house.
The luggage was stacked in the back of the van.
Joe drove, his father and Jason sat in the front on
the bench seat, and Edna and Liz were in back.
Joe's folks peppered the conversation with hometown news. But Liz knew the moment of reckon-
ing would come later; Joe's family couldn't help
but be curious about Jason calling their son
Daddy.

When Liz first glimpsed the Michaelses' imposing two-story structure, with its second-floor balcony overlooking the winding creek, the valley, and the mountains, she forgot her worries. She fell in love with the house immediately. It looked so inviting with its green shutters and green-and-white wicker furniture on the porch. Off to the side, between two mighty oaks, hung a hammock.

"I spent many nights on that hammock." Joe caught Liz's eye in the rearview mirror. As they made their way up the long tree-lined drive he told Jason, "This is where I grew up. I caught trout in that stream."

"Wow! It's neat." Jason breathed, awestruck.

Wow! is right, thought Liz, who was falling under the spell too.

"Food for the soul and the body," said Vernon.

Liz walked up the stairs, pausing to breathe the clean air, see the rushing stream. Joe came up behind her.

"The stream swells to twice its width during the spring thaw." Joe's breath was near her cheek. Around Joe there'd never be a thaw—because there'd never be a freeze. She turned her attention to the spectacular view of Pikes Peak, the snowcapped Rocky Mountains.

Jason jabbed his finger. "Did you really climb Pikes Peak?"

Joe balanced Jason on the railing, careful to keep his cast at a comfortable angle. "Yes, but my brother and I prefer riding a horse up the Barr National Recreation Trail."

Jason immediately declared he wanted to ride a horse up the trail too. "Mommy, this is swell. Now I can learn to fish and ride right here. Then I'm going to climb the mountain, scream, and hear my echo," he announced grandly.

Joe ruffled the boy's hair. "You won't be ready to climb for a while, sport. How about settling for the Pikes Peak Cog Railway instead?" He went on to explain it was neat to reach the top that way too.

"Daddy, will Mommy come too?"

Joe captured Liz's gaze and softly said, "Yes."

One of these days he was going to force Liz to really think about the two of them. Liz had become a part of him, holding him to her in countless ways. He wasn't about to give up.

Edna walked up behind them, and Liz felt her cheeks burning. She took Edna aside. "Please don't pay any attention to Jason calling Joe Daddy earlier. It's just a phase he's going through. I'll explain later."

Edna squeezed her hand in acknowledgement. "Jason, how would you like some milk and cookies after that long plane ride?" Jason didn't have to be asked twice.

"Come on, Liz, I'll give you a tour of the house," Joe said.

The interior was designed like a traditional colonial home, with the staircase separating the havles of the house. The first floor consisted of a white-and-blue-tiled kitchen, a living room with splashes of yellows, browns, and white, a baby grand in front of a picture window, a large country dining room with an oval table that sat twelve, two bathrooms, a utility room, and a pantry, its shelves stocked with mason jars of Edna's home-grown fruits and vegetables.

"Dad and Mom built an addition downstairs so Dad wouldn't have to climb the stairs if his arthritis is bothering him," Joe told Liz. Then he led her down a hall and into a sunny room. "Here's where we'll be broadcasting the show."

Liz made a slow circle. She smiled. "Joe, it's marvelous." In the center of the airy sun parlor was a large, round, glass-topped table with chairs. Chintz-covered chairs with ottomans, a sofa, and many hanging and standing plants completed the cheerful room.

"I've spoken with our technician, Pete Keeting. He's checked out the place, and there won't be any problem." Then he added, "I'm the only one with a problem."

Liz sent him a look of concern. "Joe, are you ill?"

"You might say that," he said cautiously, lowering his voice. Dammit, he wanted to scream from the rafters, Liz Davis is mine. Yet he had no right to—not yet. But he was working on it.

Her hand immediately went to his forehead, checking his temperature. "Not there," he said, meaningfully.

Liz poked his ribs, relaxing. "I thought we weren't going to tempt fate."

He bumped against her, letting her feel the fate he had in store for her. "I lied. I want you. Come with me."

He led her to a small room off the porch that was used as a catchall. He locked the door behind them. Before she could protest he dipped his head, catching the bottom of her lip between his teeth.

Swiveling in his arms, she warned him to behave himself. "You know what happens when we get like this."

"I'm counting on it," he said huskily. The afternoon sun washed in through the one small window, highlighting them in the center. "Now relax. You can see the house anytime; it's not going away. Besides, Jason's getting his nourishment. I want mine."

"You're a beast," she chuckled, snuggling up to him, ready to nourish him.

"Yeah," he agreed, settling down to business.

"Joe?" she whispered into his mouth.

He lifted his head from a kiss he was just beginning to enjoy. "What is it?"

"You've got to speak to your parents about Jason calling you Daddy." She pressed her lips to his, tracing the outline with her tongue. "Joe?"

"Now what?" His voice was half-moan, half-groan.

"You won't forget?"

He licked the side of her neck. "Quiet, woman. We don't have all day in here. How many cookies can a kid eat?"

His mouth found hers in a soft, lingering kiss. It felt wonderful. His tongue slipped through the barrier of her teeth, and for a while they explored to their hearts' content. Then Liz floated back to earth with a sigh, as all of a sudden what they were doing and where they were doing it hit her.

"Joe, we'd better join the others." He waited while she straightened her clothes.

"I could get used to this," he murmured softly in her ear. "What about you?"

Her fingers slid gently through his hair. "Making out? You bet." But she knew it wasn't what he meant. She wasn't ready to deal with the real question lurking behind his teasing.

They slipped back into the kitchen. No one seemed to have noticed their absence. "We're going upstairs. Jason said he wanted to go too," Edna said.

Over Jason's protests, Joe carried him to the second floor rather than let him try to attempt the steps. The second floor had a wide center hallway with bedrooms on either side. At each end of the hall was a bathroom. Edna pointed to the balcony.

"It's the most romantic spot to watch the lovely sunsets," Edna said, slipping her hand into Vernon's.

Liz smiled at them. Why couldn't Joe own a toy store? Then he'd never have to travel, she could settle down, and they could be a real family. "Your house is wonderful," she said. "It's like an old-fashioned farmhouse with modern conveniences."

Edna smiled. "That's exactly how we envisioned it. We knew we wanted to stay here the rest of our lives, so we went ahead and did it right the first time."

The front door opened, to the boisterous hellos of Tom and his family. At the last minute Tom decided he and Joe had too much catching up to do to wait for another day. While the men chatted Liz helped Frances set the dining room table. For dinner Edna ladled out portions of hearty beef stew and dumplings. Thick slices of warm, home-made baked bread was used for dunking. For dessert Edna served warm apple pie à la mode. As the talk flowed back and forth Joe surreptitiously kept an eye on Liz, wondering what she made of his exuberant clan.

Finally Jason rubbed his eyes, yawning. "I think it's time for bed, Jason," Joe said as naturally as if he were his father.

"Mom," Mike asked Frances, "Can I stay over too?"

Then the miracle of childhood happened. As soon as Frances gave Mike permission to spend the night, Jason got his second wind. Whooping with glee, the boys eagerly scrambled away from the table—Jason thumping with his crutches, Mike sprinting. Liz was grateful to Frances for her thoughtfulness, believing it was prompted by wanting Jason to feel comfortable on his first night in a strange house. With a maple bunk bed in the room the boys were going to share, there was no chance of his being lonely.

For once Jason couldn't wait to go to bed; he was dying to sleep in a bunk bed, even if it was only the lower bunk. Liz and Frances oversaw the boys' nightly rituals and listened to them plan all the good times they were going to have during the summer.

Frances returned to the others, but Liz opted to remain upstairs a while longer to unpack her suitcases. Joe came up a few minutes later, offering to help. "You should have told me about the picture in the newspaper when I asked you, Joe."

"I didn't want you to back out of coming here, Liz." Before she could protest he took her face in his hands, crushing her mouth to his. Their lips caressing, their tongues touching, he slipped his arm around her waist.

The worry faded as his lips pressed her throat. She began to giggle.

"What's so funny?" he asked.

"All that time in the hospital room I thought the little rascal was sleeping." She turned crimson, remembering how intensely he'd kissed her one day. "Oh my!"

Joe grinned, his hands skimming over her curves. "Shows you what *we* know." He moved to bring her tight against him, lifting her hips. Groaning, he lowered his mouth to hers, muttering, "Being under the same roof with you isn't such a good idea. Kissing is definitely out."

She munched his lip. "Good rule . . . We'll start later."

"Much later," he muttered, attending to business.

She broke away. "Joe, have you any idea why you're doing this?"

"Doing what?"

"Kissing me every chance you get." She wasn't complaining, but Joe seemed to be on some sort of a campaign.

He gripped her arms, holding her away, his eyes dark with meaning. "Do you have to ask me? One of these days we need to talk about us."

He saw the curtain drop. The cool reserve she used when he ventured too close. Liz Davis, actress/mother, returned center stage in all her protective glory—cool; elegant; aloof. The veil drawn. She would give herself to him to love, but she wouldn't allow herself to love him enough to take a chance. Annoyed, he let her go, sweeping his hand through his hair in frustration.

Liz looked in the closet for a hanger. "It might

be better if we cooled off, didn't repeat scenes like this."

Joe's eyes hardened. He met her look with an impassive expression. "Strictly business."

She tilted her head. He'd seen her television character adopt the same defiant gesture hundreds of times. Come no closer, it said.

"The trouble with you, Liz, is you demand guarantees. Life's not like that. You have nothing to worry about; the sooner we get back to business, the better. Oh, by the way, Shirley Richards is scheduled to be our first guest."

"Not that piranha!" Liz cried.

"The same," he said smoothly. "I suggest you draw in your claws. This isn't personal, it's business: She agreed to stop on her way to the Coast."

"How about what *I* agreed?" snapped Liz. "Why wasn't I consulted?"

"Forget it, Liz, it's too late to throw a fit."

"I never throw fits—I'm a professional."

"Then act like a professional. Neither one of us was consulted. Shirley smelled a story and was willing to make a stop here. Her people contacted the radio station and they contacted my agent. It isn't necessary to turn this into a three-ring circus."

After he left she collapsed in a chair, stewing. What had she let herself in for? She should have rented a house in the area. There was no place to hide here.

"Hi, can you stand company while you unpack?" A smiling Frances entered the room. Liz sent her a weak smile. How much had she overheard?

"Right now, Fran, I'll take any kind gesture I can get."

"Kind gesture number one: helping you unpack." Frances efficiently dealt with the contents of a suitcase, most of which contained Jason's favorite books and stuffed animals.

"Joe passed me in the hall. I can't say he was full of good cheer, either."

Liz grunted.

"Do you want to talk about it?"

"We'll work it out. It's pre-show jitters."

Frances hung up the blue sequin. "This is some dress. I hope you have a place to wear it."

"I hope so too. I couldn't resist bringing it."

"It's perfect. You can wear it to celebrate."

"Celebrate what?" she asked gloomily.

"Making up. Whenever Tom and I have a serious fight we celebrate to make up. It won't do to have Mommy and Daddy fighting, will it?"

"Don't pay any attention to Jason. He was just trying to get a reaction," Liz said.

"Me?" The smile on Frances's face betrayed her. "Why should I think two beautiful people who spend most of their time making love to one another on television might also be attracted to each other after hours? Certainly I'm not foolish enough to believe the picture I saw of you two in a clinch to end all clinches. Newspapers always lie, don't they? As to Joe's being called Daddy . . . I kinda like the sound of it. It's the *reason* why Jason calls Joe Daddy that needs investigating."

Liz knew she needed a friend, a woman friend, and Frances seemed like someone she could confide in. "The problem is Joe and I operate from different viewpoints, different philosophies. I want to live my life one way and Joe—"

Fran interrupted. "Joe wants to meet life head-on, try new avenues. Take his chances. Go where the action is. A go-for-it kind of approach. Provided he's thoroughly checked both sides of the issue. Once he makes up his mind it's hard to budge him. Doesn't that sum it up?"

"How did you know?"

Frances leaned against the chest of drawers. "I married his brother. If ever a mother gave birth to two peas in a pod, it's Edna."

Liz gave a peach dirndl skirt a shake. "You met Tom when he was in med school, didn't you?"

"No. That's probably one of the few things Joe wasn't let in on in the beginning of my relationship with Tom. We met when I was married to my first husband."

Surprised, Liz looked up. "You were married before? I didn't know."

"I was widowed. There's no need to hide it—or advertise it either for that matter. My first husband was in the Air Force, stationed at the academy here in the Springs. Tom flies recreationally; so did Gordo. They met, became buddies. It's funny—I used to worry Gordo might be hurt flying jets. I wasn't happy about living on various bases, always having to set up a new house, find a different nursing position. You see, I thought it would be too hard on Janice having her father away so much."

"Janice isn't Tom's daughter?" Liz asked.

Frances sat down. She pushed a hand through her hair, as if searching for the right words. "Not biologically, no, but you couldn't find a more devoted father anywhere than Tom. Janice knows about her father; he was a good, fine man who loved her. She has grandparents we see from Gordo's side of the family. We keep Gordo as a loved and distant memory, part of our past. Tom's her father now, the man who'll be there for her as she grows up."

"What happened?" Liz asked quietly.

"He was in a fatal car accident when Janice was two."

Frances lifted shining eyes, her voice faltering. "After . . . after . . . well, Tom was there whenever I needed him. I don't have to tell you how alone you feel, how it seems everything in the world suddenly is counted by two's, like on Noah's ark. I was miserable and had a young child who was as confused as I was."

"I never knew how Tom figured out when things were getting too much for me, but he did. He'd come over. I'd rant and rave. One day I stopped and took a good look at the man whose chest I'd been beating for months. Gradually I fell in love with him. He told me he'd been in love with me the whole time. There's never been a man as good as Tom; I'd follow him to the ends of the earth." She stopped and looked at her hands. "Liz, I don't usually tell my story to people."

Liz went to her, her eyes as misty as Frances's. "Why did you tell me?" she asked as she hugged the other woman.

"I'm a survivor, Liz, and so are you," Frances said. "From a practical viewpoint, I think women have it harder than men. You've carved out a successful career; you're a loving mother. This might not be true for all women, but I believe life's not complete unless there's someone to share it with. I know Joe, know he's as good a man as his brother is. In time I hope to know you well too. And sometimes it's good to hear the other side of the story from one who's lived through it."

"Then perhaps you can appreciate why I don't see my future in a situation where travel can separate Jason from a father and me from a husband. Joe is a very handsome man, I'm sure he'd have a lot of temptation."

Frances smiled. "Joe always played the field. Perhaps he's never fallen in love before."

Maybe he still hadn't! Liz thought.

When the two women came back downstairs, they overheard Joe's deep voice. "You don't know the half of it," he was saying. "Jason's part con man, part angel. He started calling me Daddy, then made a pact with me to call me Uncle Joe when we got to Colorado. You heard him at the airport. Now he's calling you Grandpa and Grandma."

Vernon puffed his pipe. "That little fella's about as smart as Janice was. Do you recall those days, Edna?"

"How can I forget? Janice's as smart as she's beautiful. She gets it from her mother."

"My daughter gets her brains from me," Tom declared, ending all doubts, nodding to Fran and Liz.

"Liz," Vernon said, "Joe tells me you do some writing."

She looked at Joe in amazement as she sat down beside him.

"How did you know that, Joe? I never told you; I never told anyone." The scripts she'd written were relegated to her bottom drawer.

His eyes became very sober. "Jason told me." He's also told me other things, Joe thought to himself, like how much he wants me to be his daddy.

"Jason's got a big mouth," she muttered, wondering what else Jason confided in Joe about. Her writing was strictly therapeutic. Many an evening she and her son sat side by side on the sofa, Jason practicing his letters, she toiling away at her script, her replacement for another adult.

"I think it's exciting," Tom said.

Joe changed the subject. "I bet none of you guessed the writers for our show live in California, Chicago, and Texas." They hadn't, and were filled with questions.

"It's not complicated. It's done by conference-calling and fax machines," Liz explained, pondering the subject of Joe's love life. The man was shameless, eating her up with those Paul Newman eyes in front of everyone as if she'd paraded into the room naked.

"In other words," Edna said, "a writer may live anywhere he or she chooses."

"That's right," Liz said.

"Including Colorado Springs?" Vernon asked.

"Sure," said Joe, keeping his eyes on Liz.

Liz picked up a fork, pretending great interest in its design.

"Tell me more about the Springs," Liz prompted.

All the Michaelses were only too happy to discuss their growing metropolis. Tom and Fran adored living in Colorado Springs and couldn't understand how people settled elsewhere, but were just as happy they did.

Liz heard about a place with the exotic name of the Garden of the Gods, a 940-acre park with fascinating rock formations and a restaurant in town where the waiters poured coffee over their shoulders into a cup and saucer held behind their backs.

"We never tell this story in front of the kids. We're afraid it might tempt them to try it too."

Joe had kept his mind on the topic. It wasn't easy. For the first time in his life, he'd found a woman he wanted to marry, and now that he was anxious to be led to the altar, he couldn't budge her!

"Liz," he said after a while, "I've explained to the folks why Jason's been calling me Daddy."

She glanced quickly around the table, receiving reassurances. "I'm glad you understand. It's just a phase; it'll pass," she added.

Joe's lips tightened. He hated hearing himself spoken of as *just a phase*. Annoyed, he rose from the table to get a drink. Maybe this would make a terrific episode for their soap opera characters, but in real life it stank!

The evening ended with hugs and promises to return soon. Edna and Vernon Michaels called out "good night" as Liz mounted the staircase.

"Is there anything you need?" Joe asked Liz as he halted at the top of the landing. He wasn't happy, and he didn't care if she knew it.

She'd been dreading saying good night to him, so she did what she did best—groped around for a safe subject. Ever since they'd become lovers their good nights were long, lingering, lovely. She ached to feel his arms surround her tonight.

"Joe, Frances told me about her first marriage, about Tom's not being Janice's father."

"Biological father, you mean. She's his, believe me." His shrug was eloquent. "But that doesn't change anything between us, does it? How did you put it downstairs? Oh yes, I'm *just a phase.*"

She stepped back as if he'd slapped her, a chill replacing her warmth. She was drained from the day. She wanted to be cherished, to be protected; mostly she wanted to see his teasing smile.

"Yes," she said.

He drew back. Life would be a lot simpler without Liz. It would also be unthinkable. From down the hall they heard Jason calling his mother to take him to the bathroom.

"Good night, Liz. I'll see you in the morning. We've got a lot of work ahead of us."

To her surprise, Liz slept like a log.

She awoke to heavy breathing and smothered, high-pitched giggles. She popped open an eye to find two little boys playfully nudging each other.

"She's awake," Jason declared, bringing his face so close that Liz threw her arm around his neck, kissing him. Mike, not to be outdone, checked to make sure, getting the same treatment.

"Hurry up, Mommy. Grandma's got breakfast on the table and Grandpa says he's going to eat yours."

"He did not," Mike objected.

"Did too," Jason said, elbowing his way in.

"My foot!" Mike shouted.

They were on their way to a great friendship.

Mumbling that it wasn't fair, Liz sat up, rubbing the sleep from her eyes. She wore a sheer pale blue gown, the strap of which had fallen off her shoulder. Her blond hair was mussed. Pushing both hands through it, she yawned. "Cut that out, both of you. Jason, who tied your shoelaces? For that matter, who dressed you? Did you wash?"

Jason gleefully pointed to the man leaning against the doorjamb. "Daddy dressed me. I brushed my teeth. Both sides." Tucking two fingers into the ends of his mouth, he bared his teeth, giving her his best horse grin. "See?"

Pride prevented Liz from patting the mattress and inviting Joe to sit down. He looked so good, so inviting. She slanted him a look. "Thanks."

"You're welcome." He saw the pride, the damnable pride, in her face. "Hurry up," he said gruffly. "We let you sleep late today."

With that he turned on his heel and left. Jason clumped after him. Mike zipped past.

"Up you go, son," she heard Joe say.

Damn him. She flung her pillow at the door. She rose from the bed. "Ouch!" she yelled, tripping over the hem of her gown. She fell to the floor, more surprised than hurt, cursing her luck.

"What happened to you?" Joe was by her side, scowling. His face was a thundercloud. None too gently, he cupped her chin, forcing her to look at him. When he saw the spitfire look in her eyes, the creamy tops of her breasts exposed by the way she'd fallen, he felt his breath quicken. She made him quiver with desire. He sat back on his haunches, grumbling. "Geez, I can't leave either of you for a minute. What did you do now?"

Tears smarted her eyes. Did he think her a complete dolt? Why was it that whenever Joe was around she folded, became putty? Warm mush!

She yanked up the strap on her gown. "Nothing happened. I like it down here and thought I'd try it."

He glared at her. "Good. Then stay down there."

"Joe, help me up!"

"Give me one good reason."

"I'm hurt."

He knew she wasn't. "It's just a passing phase. You'll get over it."

"Damn you, help me up. If you don't, you do the talk show yourself—both parts. I'll grow old and wrinkled on the floor. Everyone will have to step over me. I'll mold. You'll have Jason on your hands the rest of your life; then where will you be?"

"Suppose you figure out the answer to that question!" he said, heaving her up unceremoniously. But she was so glad he hadn't left that she didn't care if he yelled at her.

"Where did you come from? I thought you went downstairs with Jason."

"I did," he said, feeling her tender ankle. "Jason forgot a book he wants to read to Dad. I swear, between the two of you invalids, a man can't have a moment's peace."

"Oh, Joe," she said, "I'm such an absolute jerk sometimes. Bear with me, please."

He eyed her suspiciously. Liz Davis wouldn't

call herself a jerk under *any* circumstances. The words must have come from an old script.

He planted his hands low on his hips. "Why should I?"

She moved her shoulders in such a way that it thrust her body forward, her breasts straining the material of her gown. "Because I asked."

He knew he was sunk. She did it to him every time. His deep blue eyes took on a teasing glow. "Touch me," he commanded softly.

A ripple of pleasure went through her. Her fingers didn't know where to go first, so they went to his face. She brushed a lock of his hair from his forehead. He was so grumpy, so adorable; she wanted to touch him to her heart's content. "Mmmmm, that's better," he said. "I want to touch too."

Her eyes grew wide. "It's not safe."

He leered at her. "I don't mean it to be."

"We'd better not," she laughed. "You know what happened downstairs."

"Nothing happened. You were chicken." He glanced up to see if the door was closed.

"Go away," she said, weakly. His arms looped about her waist.

"Come on, Liz, nobody's watching."

"You dog," she mumbled, reaching for him again.

She felt him tremble as his mouth closed over hers. His hand found her breast, cupping it in a way he knew excited her. Through the thin gown she strained toward him. This was where she wanted to be, in the arms of the man who excited her as no other. He kissed her so thoroughly she felt warm and quivery.

"That's enough for now," he said, sauntering away. His voice sounded husky. Laughing, he trundled off in the direction of the door. "Hurry up," he called over his shoulder.

"You beast!" she shouted. She narrowly missed hitting him with the pillow she threw at him.

Joe headed for the bathroom to splash cold water on his face. He'd had a long talk with Tom earlier. Tom's advice had been to shower Liz with attention. "Drive her nuts. She'll end up so crazy about you she'll see she had nothing to worry about. Thinking about your traveling lifestyle will be the furthest thing from her mind," he'd said.

Joe tried Tom's advice. The trouble was, in the process *he* was clearly going nuts. He wanted Liz; a lot of good it did him. He was stuck in his parents' home, Jason still called him Daddy, and Liz was willing to call him lover.

But not husband.

The main condition of her surrender was total capitulation on his part, Joe thought to himself. The man she'd marry would have to stay put. Period. Her ideas about what was best for Jason ruled her.

He wondered if being around his family would work for him or against him. Last night they'd all said they could never think of living anywhere other than the Springs. Tom and Fran had a happy life; so did his parents. Yet he knew without a doubt that his mother and Fran would follow their husbands to the ends of the earth, would wait at home if need be, without the demons Liz carried.

He also knew it wasn't wise to press Liz. Could

he really blame her for her attitude, her staunch belief in the life she felt was best for her and her son? Probably not, if he were honest. What young mother in her position wouldn't be scared? So it all came down to guarantees.

Liz dressed, then came downstairs to slip into the chair opposite Joe in the sun room. She gave him a brilliant smile, tilted her head, and acted as if nothing had happened upstairs.

Later, Edna found them going through piles of magazine articles, newspaper clippings, and notes. "I didn't want to disturb you while you were busy," she said, "so I told the lady I'd give you the message."

"What lady?" Joe asked, frowning at the interruption. Keeping his thoughts straight was hard enough with Liz shuffling around in the seat near him. She had doused herself with his favorite perfume.

"Shirley Richards is at the Broadmoor Hotel."

"Terrific. She's three days early." Liz's mood soured immediately.

Joe put down his pen. "Is that any way to talk about our first guest?"

"It's the *kindest* way to talk about her."

"Cheer up," Joe urged. "Nothing could top the picture in the paper. The interview will be a piece of cake."

Liz sulked. Her sixth sense sent out all kinds of warnings. If there was one person on the face of the earth who caused more trouble than she was worth, it was that big mouthed gossip Shirley Richards.

"Where's your backbone, Liz?" Joe taunted.

She stiffened. "Do you think I'm spineless?" He shrugged. Spineless. It was a powerful word. Is that how Joe saw her? Worse still, maybe he was right. Well, Shirley wasn't going to make a frightened rabbit out of her! Not by a long shot.

"Joe, you're right. I have nothing to fear from that woman. This time I have the mike," Liz announced, patting the microphone. Joe knew she was pysching herself for the interview. "Nothing's going to happen unless I allow it. For once the Shirley jinx isn't going to work."

For good luck she crossed her fingers.

As it turned out, she should have crossed her toes too.

Nine

At Joe and Edna's urging, Vernon agreed to put a help-wanted ad in the local paper. Two women with toy-merchandising experience called for interviews. "But I'm still going back to work part-time, Edna," Vernon said, the look in his eye saying, "I dare you to stop me!"

"Dad'll be fine, Mom," Joe said, hunting for the keys to the car to drive Vernon into town. "Come on, son." Jason's face lit up the room.

"Right, Dad." Liz shook her head. So much for the mother-and-son talk she'd had with Jason that morning. As the car left the driveway she stood for a moment, thinking of the three generations of men heading toward town. Jason's little head was bobbing from one man to the other. She knew he was talking up a storm, and knew Joe was getting a big kick out of it.

It was Jason's first trip to the toy store, and when he returned he was over the moon. "Liz,"

Joe said proudly, "you should have seen him. Jason didn't know where to look first. If he wasn't on crutches he'd have been racing up and down the aisles. Dad gave him permission to pick any toy he wanted."

Liz fretted. The more Joe and his family went out of their way to be nice, the guiltier she felt.

And Joe and Jason were becoming best buddies, playing Nintendo games, laughing, or arguing over a point. Edna had her special time with the boy too. Usually it was while she baked cookies. Jason would perch on a stool, helping to roll out dough, flour on his face and shirt, gabbing with his "Grandma."

"What do you think, Liz? Is Jason fitting right in this family or what?"

She nodded. "I think your parents are wonderful, but they're much too generous."

In repayment, Liz decided to order a new recliner for Vernon, a convection-microwave oven for Edna.

"Jason's giving Dad a lot of pleasure, keeping him company. Let him have some pleasure too."

Liz gave a disapproving cluck. "I know, but—"

Joe ended her argument with a quick kiss, as much to cheer himself up as to shut her up. "No buts, Liz, Jason's family." Which is exactly what she was concerned about.

In two days their first program began. Liz noticed Joe spent a lot of time on the phone. But when she asked him about it, he said he was taking care of personal business.

Which he was. His plans to find a property to produce had led to a series of discussions with the broadcasting company. If, after the show with Liz, Joe wanted to produce and package another talk show, the contract was his. He decided not to mention this to Liz. He thought it wouldn't change anything, since he was still in a profession where the two of them could be separated.

The two of them were in the sun room, going over ideas. She rubbed the back of her neck, relieving the crick in it.

Joe came around to her. "I've got a much better way to relieve tension," he said, pulling her into his arms.

As always, all Joe had to do was use his teasing voice and hers would drop to a low, husky pitch. "For starters, if you're going to kiss me you should pull the shade down on the door."

"Suppose I lock it too?" he said roughly, gazing into her soft, brown eyes. "Then what can I do? I miss you. I miss us. It's time we had a serious talk."

Her heart hammering, Liz gave him the only answer possible. "Nothing's changed, Joe. This is a summer hiatus. Let's enjoy it while we can."

His face took on a stubborn look. "That's where you're dead wrong, Liz. Everything's changed, only you're too blind to notice." He stormed out of the room, banging the door for anyone within earshot to hear.

Liz flinched. Their "discussions" were becoming louder and louder. Darn the man. She had to stick to her guns, for Jason's sake. It might be different if their careers allowed them to live in one place. Why did it have to end this way, she thought wearily, when all she wanted to do was to make love to him?

She knew Edna had noticed their squabbles. And when Liz entered the kitchen, she found Joe's mother gazed thoughtfully at her.

"Funny thing about men," Edna said without preamble. "If I've learned one thing in all my years of marriage, it's that a smart woman should never try to keep an active man down. Or in one place. Another thing I learned is that a good man is hard to find."

Liz understood the subtle message. She mentioned this to Frances when the two women took the boys to a drive-in for hamburgers a few hours later.

Frances munched on a french fry. "It's Edna's way of protecting her son. She did the same thing with me."

"You'd never know it," Liz said.

"Because Tom's happy."

Liz sipped her soda. "In other words, Edna thinks Joe's not happy and it's my fault. How depressing."

At the next table a father berated his son for a minor infraction. Liz thought about Joe, how gentle he was with Jason.

"Don't jump to conclusions, Liz," Fran advised. "Edna's an astute woman. She likes you."

Liz brought her attention back to their table. "How do you know she doesn't think I'm just a shallow actress turning her son's head?"

"For one thing, you don't act like one. For another, she told me she likes you."

"Did she also tell you how she'd feel about Joe taking on another man's family?"

Frances heard the hopeful note in Liz's voice. She smiled and reached over to squeeze her hand. "She never minded with Tom and me, so why should she object with you? Are you beginning to have second thoughts?" Liz dropped her eyes.

"You *are* reconsidering!" Fran declared happily. "That's wonderful. Have you told Joe?"

"Heavens, no!" Liz replied, sorry she hadn't denied Fran's conclusion. "We don't talk about marriage. I don't let him."

Frances was stunned. "Why not?"

Liz shrugged. Joe had come close more than once, but she'd steered him in another direction. "It's just a theory. I think if I discuss marriage with him and we can't come to terms, I'll know it's over. This is all so new for me. Maybe I'm afraid of losing what we have."

"But you're in love with him, aren't you?"

Liz nodded. She'd been falling in love with Joe for so long she couldn't remember a time he wasn't in her thoughts. "Please don't tell him or Tom. I'm still trying to work all this out in my mind."

Frances gave her an affectionate pat. "I know, Liz. Don't wait too long, though. Joe's not the most patient man."

Joe told her the same thing.

He'd yelled at her to get her head screwed on right, to stop hiding behind all the damn *Off Limits* signs she'd posted all over her heart. Then he'd grabbed and kissed her, banging out of the house with such force he'd dislodged the back door from its hinges. Mortified, Liz had snuck up the stairs.

The next time they met Liz put on one of her best acts. She suggested a truce, so they could get some work done, although Joe's arguments were finally getting to her. Over breakfast and Jason's jabbering, they scanned the dailies, spotting human-interest news.

Joe disappeared every afternoon. He told her he was meeting with sponsors, town merchants, people with interesting occupations. That part was true. He was also going ahead with plans to produce other radio talk shows. He asked Liz to draw up lists of timely subjects to give to the talent coordinator.

Liz had managed to avoid Shirley Richards, but she dreaded seeing her, particularly as the guest for their first show.

"Forget her," Joe said, dismissing Liz's newest bout of apprehension. "We're ready for anything. Don't forget—we control the airwaves, not her. Isn't that what you said?"

"I know what I said." Liz wished she could speed up time so that Shirley would be here and gone. Her eyes glittered like topazes as she clenched her fists. "Mark my words, something's going to go wrong; I feel it in my bones," she predicted darkly.

Inwardly she was glad to see how well Joe handled the backstage work for their new venture. He thrived on the new challenge, meeting with people from all walks of life. Increasingly, Liz realized how absorbed he was by the managerial details.

"That's where the decision-making power is,"

he explained. "No one's handing me these lines. I like it."

She mentioned this in passing to Edna when she took a break to help the older woman. Both were growing to enjoy the conversations. To her delight, Liz discovered she and Edna got along very well.

"Oh, Joe hasn't the skin of an actor," Edna said offhandedly.

"What do you mean, 'the skin of an actor'?" Liz was shelling peas and dropping them into a colander to wash. Edna was rolling dough for strudel, a favorite of Joe's, for dessert. Through the window Joe's mother saw Vernon and Jason examining a flower.

"Everything I've read about actors always says you have to have a lasting commitment to it, the sort of drive to carry you over while you wait on tables, or starve in a garret, as long as there's the remote possibility of landing a role. Joe would never do that. He'd create a business first. That's why I say he's got the skin of a businessman. He takes after his father."

"Then why isn't Joe in business?" Liz asked.

Edna wiped her hands and took a seat near Liz. "We expected him to be heading up his own production company long before this. I was wondering if you might tell me why he extended his contract with *Happy Town*."

Feeling awkward, Liz avoided Edna's intelligent eyes. "I'm afraid I can't."

"Too bad," Edna said, her tone gently implying Liz wouldn't, not couldn't. She smiled and patted her hand. "Maybe one of these days you will. Anyway, don't concern yourself about Jason tomorrow. I'll keep him busy while you two are on the air."

Liz excused herself to return to the sun room. She found Joe still working. Hearing her enter, he eased back in the chair. Her face was radiant. He thought of their future. Did they have a future? He certainly hoped so. He laughed to himself. Wouldn't Shirley Richards have loved a party line to his private thoughts!

"Liz, you're a disturbing witch." He pulled her onto his lap and kissed her.

"Joe! Your mother—"

"Will approve. But just in case you're worried, when she's busy in the kitchen she rarely comes in here. Besides, she knows we're working."

"In that case, do your worst."

"How about if I do my best?" With a laugh, he pulled her mouth to his, kissing her thoroughly.

"The skin of a businessman, huh?" she murmured near his lips.

He held her at arm's length, peering down at her. "What's gotten into you? What were you and my mother talking about?" he asked, suspicion written on his handsome visage.

"You," she said happily.

Liz looped her arms around his neck, effectively ruining all pretense of getting any work done. "Quit that or we're going to find a motel to finish this."

"No, we're not. I want to talk."

"About what?" He munched a sensitive spot near the base of her throat.

Liz squirmed, forcing herself to stay with the

topic. "Your mother was saying you don't have the skin of an actor, that you have the skin of a businessman. Is that true?"

"What difference does it make?" he asked guardedly.

"It just might solve our problems," Liz said blithely. "Don't you think it would?"

He deliberately took her arms from around his neck. His cool, remote voice ground out the answer. "Sorry, Liz, I'm not the sort of man to give guarantees I can't keep. If I were, I could have saved myself a lot of time and effort."

Liz looked at him, stunned at the harshness of his tone. "I'm sure you could have," she said with biting sarcasm. One of these days she'd learn not to lead with her heart. "You'll excuse me. It's time for Jason's sponge bath."

With a heavy heart, he watched her go. Hungrily, he gazed at her slender form, her fluid curves, yearning to make love to her, wanting her so badly he flung his pencil to the other side of the room rather than call her back. If she loved him, it had to be for the right reasons—she had to love him for himself, not his job site.

The big day dawned full of early-morning promise: The weather was clear, the air crisp. They were as ready as they'd ever be. Jason played outside near Vernon, who opted not to go to work that day. "Too much going on here," he announced. They were expecting Tom and his family later. Everyone wanted to be in on the special day.

A huge bouquet of lavender and white daisies arrived from the station. Edna baked a batch of chocolate cookies and a rum cake. Liz toyed with the idea of eating the entire cake after seeing how much rum Edna put into it. She needed fortification to keep from taking potshots at Shirley, who arrived in a white stretch limousine, alighting from the automobile with an entourage: A photographer, an ad agency executive, the local district manager of the newspaper chain that printed her column, and bringing up the rear, Shirley's private secretary.

This certainly didn't look like a simple stopover on the way to the Coast, Liz thought grimly.

Edna set the table in the dining room, using her best china and sterling-silver service. A gracious hostess, she offered refreshments to everyone; Shirley declined.

"I never eat while I'm working," she said in her husky voice. "Food lulls my concentration. I'm liable to get too comfortable, miss something. Maybe later, Edna."

Liz rushed outside to warn Jason to stay out until the guests left. "They're not anyone you'd care to visit with, sweetie."

"What's Daddy doing?"

"Uncle Joe," she reminded him. "He's busy with me. We'll see you in a little while."

Liz found Shirley, armed with a micro-cassette tape recorder, interviewing Edna about Joe's childhood. "It's tit for tat in this business. Joe and Liz will interview me; and I'll write a piece on it. My column is carried by over five hundred newspapers and all the top magazines."

Don't I know it! Liz thought.

Joe almost choked as Edna painted a picture of a saintly child who never gave his parents the slightest trouble. Shirley dug deep, but Edna was unflappable. Liz wanted to hug her.

From the moment Shirley had swept through the front door, swathed in a ranch mink over her haute couture dress, Liz's premonition of doom had grown stronger.

Joe called a halt to the interview with Edna. "That's it. Show time." He propelled Liz into the room, guiding her with his hand at her waist. When Shirley wasn't looking he patted Liz's bottom, laughing when she slid into the chair so fast she rattled the mike. "Sorry," he said innocently.

Joe and Liz sat at opposite sides of a round table. Shirley sat between them. All had microphones. When given the signal, Joe smoothly began. As the introductory music faded into the background, Joe introduced himself and Liz, who then said a few welcoming words. It was the only scripted portion of the show. Joe informed the audience he and Liz would be their hosts over the next several months.

Liz introduced several sponsors. Then she spoke highly of a local singer scheduled to be tomorrow's guest. She sat quietly as Joe launched into a big buildup for Shirley Richards—"who needs no introduction," he added.

So far so good. Liz checked the time. Twenty-five minutes to go. Shirley talked about *Happy Town*. Joe and Liz exchanged swift glances. During her segment, Liz questioned Shirley about her beginnings as a columnist, her career now and so on.

"I've had a lot of luck and a sharp eye and ear," Shirley cooed, her eyes as sharp as ever. "Many of us see and hear but don't act on it. I do. In return I give my readers pleasure—which, by the way, doesn't hurt my bank account."

I bet it doesn't! Liz thought to herself.

Liz glanced at the clock. Twenty minutes. With time out for commercials. So far so good.

Eighteen minutes. Liz wiped her sweaty palms on her skirt under the table, out of Shirley's eye.

Shirley began to ask a question. "Not on this show, Shirl," Joe laughed. "You're the guest. We're the hosts."

The audience couldn't see Shirley's reaction. "Forgive me. It's this nose for news."

Liz wanted to break it.

A two-minute news break, balanced by two commercials.

Ten minutes. Liz eased up. Joe smoothly took over. He asked Shirley about the cast of the show at the Broadmoor. "What do you think of its chances to make it to Broadway?"

She smiled, then replied in a sexy undertone. "You'd make a wonderful Ray Hunter. You should have tried out for the role." She paused. "But then all your experience has been playing opposite Liz. The picture of you two in the paper was a classic."

No one had to ask which picture. Shirley had nailed him. Liz squirmed, clenching and unclenching her fists.

"Let's get back to you," Liz said, cutting in smoothly. "I've always been interested in women who have been married five times."

Joe choked back a grunt. He covered for Liz.

"What Liz means is she's fascinated by you." He glared at her, praying she'd get the message.

"Really. Well, I'll be happy to give her a few pointers," Shirley said, spreading her upper lip over her teeth. Shirley was nobody's fool.

Two more commercials. Pete Keeting gave them the high sign. All was well from his end. Liz wished she could say the same. She excused herself during the last commercial to get a cold drink of water. Quickly glancing outside, she confirmed that Jason was safely out of the way.

She slipped back into the sun room, resuming her place at the round table. With professional ease she segued into the next portion of the show, chatting with Shirley about fashion in the cinema. The segment went well. Shirley contributed fascinating information. Liz relaxed.

Three minutes. One commercial.

Almost over.

Jason banged into the room, his voice screeching excitedly. "Mommy, where's Grandma Edna? Grandpa says it's the biggest deer he's ever seen. Daddy, you come see it too."

Shirley swiveled in her seat like a windup toy gone wild. "Joe, is this child yours?"

"No!" and "Yes!" they said at the same time.

Shirley had hit pay dirt. "Which is it? Are you two married or what?"

"No."

"Yes."

"Darlings," she drawled. "You're mixing me up."

"We're getting married," Liz blurted, stunned by what she'd just said. How could she have done such a thing? She and Joe hadn't settled anything. He didn't know she'd begun to reconsider.

Joe saw the misery in her eyes. He was careful to hide his elation. Loving her, he knew she was upset and his heart went out to her. "It's all planned," Joe said smoothly. "Jason is Liz's son. We think of each other as family."

Shirley clucked, making no effort to hide her mounting excitement. She took a quick read of the emotional pulse in the room.

"I can't tell you how glad I am to be here. Imagine being in on the scoop as America's nighttime soap opera sweethearts combine fantasy with reality."

Shirley hugged the mike. It sounded as if she were the hostess. "Liz darling, this is exactly what I meant by eyes and ears and opportunity."

Joe's silky voice addressed the unseen audience. If he could have put a muzzle over Shirley's mouth, he would have. Liz was as white as a sheet. He had his answer. She didn't want to marry him. She'd been embarrassed by Jason's interruption, and had said they were getting married to cover the confusion. Edna hurried into the room, scooping Jason up in her arms, his crutches banging on the floor.

"Come on, sweetie. Show Grandma the deer."

Joe slipped back into his role as host, finishing the lie Liz began. "Never a dull moment on this show, folks. Actually, there's a very simple explanation, one which I'm sure you all will find boringly commonplace. Liz and I flew out to Colorado to finalize our wedding plans. I'm sure you understand when I say living in the glare of the limelight makes us appreciate privacy at this time. Now, Shirley, let's get back to you."

Shirley simpered through the rest of the show, the cat lapping the pint of cream, purring through every last drop.

There had been crucial moments in Liz's life when she'd been called on to give an award-winning performance. But her acting skills were never more useful then now.

The show over, Liz thrust out her hand, squeezing a plastic smile onto her face. "Would you excuse me? I thought I'd go out and see Jason's deer."

She wasn't excused. Shirley held up her palms as if to say it wasn't time to shake Liz's hand. "When is this marriage taking place?" she asked.

"Next week. It's just the family. We want it to be a quiet, simple ceremony," Joe replied. He put his arm around Liz's waist, feeling her tremble with rage.

Undaunted, Shirley positioned herself in front of the screen door, blocking their way, revelling in her victory.

"I'm not leaving town without pictures of your wedding, lovely people. I wouldn't dream of cheating my readers. What with five hundred outlets, the magazines that carry my column, radio, television, the press coverage your announcement will generate, you two are going to have the wedding of the century."

"Hardly that," Joe said. "We're just plain folk who happen to be in the entertainment business. This isn't an earth-shattering event."

Shirley coolly ignored his statement. "Oh, but

you're wrong, my dears. Modesty aside, there's no way you can have a private wedding now. If I were you two I'd consider myself lucky to share your happiness."

"Shirley," Liz said smoothly, "after we're married we'll give you all the pictures you want. We are not public people; only our work is. However, we'll give you the first interview, but the wedding will be private."

So private it's not going to take place!

Ten

There was a long moment of silence following Liz's announcement of their private-ceremony nuptials.

Joe moved to fill the breach. He was worried about Liz, who looked drawn. "Shirley, Liz and I appreciate your generous offer, don't we, honey?"

"Of course," she murmured, reeling from her impulsive behavior. Joe had saved the day, going along with her as she told a whole nation her wedding plans.

She felt an inexplicable fury, as if a thousand lights were popping in her head.

Edna returned to the house with the news that the deer had run away. "Edna," Shirley trilled, "I'd adore a slice of your marvelous cake. Shame on you for holding back the news from me."

"What news?" Edna asked innocently.

"What news, she asks." Shirley winked at her secretary and her photographer. "Get a picture of this, Marvin," she ordered. "Edna, you sly fox, you know I'm talking about the upcoming wedding between Joe and Liz. Is there any other news in this house I should know about? Those adorable devils weren't going to tell me. I had to pry it out of them. Why, if it weren't for Jason I still wouldn't know—by the way, Liz, why have you been hiding your adorable youngster?"

Liz responded swiftly, shrugging her hand away from Joe's. "You understand, don't you, Shirley? I figured you aren't interested in little boys."

Edna scooted Jason and Vernon out of the house like unwanted guests. Then everyone heard car tires crunching on the gravel.

Frances piled in, with Mike and Janice in tow.

Unaware of the glacial atmosphere in the kitchen, Frances said, "Tom's leaving the hospital early today. He'll be along in half an hour. So, how did the first broadcast go? Is everybody in the mood to party?"

"You didn't hear the broadcast?" Liz asked.

"My car radio's on the blink. You must be Shirley Richards." Frances pumped her hand. "I'm so delighted to meet you. Any friend of Liz's is a friend of mine."

Joe tried to send her a message to quit, but failed. Frances blithely continued, "So what do you think of our little town?"

The phone rang. A reporter from the Gannett newspaper chain asked to speak to the happy couple. Then more entertainment reporters called.

"Tell them we're out," Joe said in a low voice to Edna. He ran upstairs to his bedroom and snatched the phone's receiver off the hook, then smothered the disconnection sound with a pillow.

"Will you excuse us?" Joe rushed back into the kitchen for Liz. If he didn't get her out of there, there was no telling what she'd do. She'd taken on the aura of her television character; while he admired her for her professionalism, the timing was all wrong.

Liz followed Joe outside. Neither said a word. Liz kept flailing her arms like a hummingbird.

"Take it easy, honey. No damage was done."

She sent him a look. "Not much. The whole nation expects us to get married."

"Is that so terrible?" he asked quietly, but Liz was too worked up to hear him, to catch his meaning. While he thought marrying Liz was a wonderful idea, she was almost in tears as she relived the scene with Shirley.

"Joe, did you hear that woman? The nerve of her. I knew it! I knew that female monster would do something. She's an alley cat."

"Liz, she's doing her job. She brought our problem out in the open. Now we'll have to deal with it. Our problem isn't with her, can't you see that?"

Liz flung his remark aside. "All I see is a woman minding my business, not hers."

He stepped back, shaking his head in disgust. He was stung by her words. "You're really something, do you know that?"

Liz kicked a pebble out of the way. "She's minding my business!"

Joe sighed, "*Your* business, not *our* business. I lied for you back there, lady! I lied for you and Jason on coast-to-coast radio. And all you can say is that Shirley Richard's a monster."

Liz tossed her head, as if the swirling of her

hair could blow away the bad moments. "What do you want me to say, dammit? That I appreciate your coming to our rescue? It seems you're doing a lot of that lately."

He felt like a frustrated fool. "Liz, I'm in love with you. I thought by now you'd have come to know that."

She lifted her eyes to see him waiting for her response. She looked at his dear face, loving each of its separate parts—his strong forehead, his nose, his eyes, his full lips, his white, even teeth.

And she looked beyond that to his soul.

"Joe." She stepped into his open arms. "I'm in love with you too. I have been for a long time."

He smiled, breathing the sweet mountain air, kissing her lips. "Then what's the problem? Why not make an honest gossip out of Shirley? Let's get married."

Liz wanted to take that final step, but couldn't. If she said yes, it would all start again. She'd made a promise to herself not to take roles that required her to be away from Jason. She couldn't ask Joe to make that same promise. It wouldn't be fair. Joe's work would take him far afield; then what? How would she react to saying good-bye to a husband on the go? Not very well. "I wish it were that simple."

He lifted her hand, kissing the palm.

"It could be."

"What about Jason?" she said, hiding like a coward behind her son.

"What about him? I love him, he loves me. I'd like to adopt him. I couldn't feel more love for him than if he had been born mine. I don't even mind skipping the diaper part."

Liz softly kissed Joe's lips. "I love you for that, Joe."

He gripped her arms. "Then why do I get the feeling you're saying good-bye instead of hello?"

She eased out of his embrace, the old fears resurfacing. Why couldn't she just say the hell with it, she'd uproot her son, follow Joe to the ends of the earth, she'd be there at the airport to send him off and welcome him home. Tears filled her eyes.

It had little to do with jobs. Her fears were more basic. She hadn't trusted her heart. She'd been so busy trying to run her life so calmly, so without risk, that she had been in danger of shriveling up emotionally. Joe had come along and changed all that.

Joe watched her go to the nearest tree and pick up a twig from the base. For a few seconds she whipped it back and forth like a pendulum.

A pendulum deciding her life.

So that's it? he thought. His eyes hardened into steel. Liz still demanded guarantees. It was risky, dangerous even to put the decision on her slim shoulders, when all he wanted to do was protect her. He'd asked himself why he hadn't taken her into his confidence, told her he was setting up a talent agency, intended to package radio shows too. The answer was simple: If it didn't work out, if he would have to resume an acting career, then what?

He put his hands on her shoulders. "Liz, don't worry about Shirley or what my family thinks. Wedding announcements have been known to be called off. Our announcement was a lie. But we can make sure it doesn't turn into one."

Tears slowly coursed down her cheeks.

"What are you saying, Joe?"

"I'm letting you off the hook before you go through the trouble of giving me all the reasons a marriage between us wouldn't work. I'm saying your love for me isn't strong enough. I wish it were. For all our sakes, it's better to end this now."

Liz lingered outside long after Joe left. Long after Shirley and her entourage left. Long after the chill of evening matched the chill in her heart, Jason came out to find her. She threw her arms around him, hugging him tightly.

"What are you going to do?" he asked, pushing her from him. She knew she had to leave this house, and she also knew Jason would never understand.

The broadcast was moved to the radio studio in town. When Joe told her about the change, she nodded it was fine with her. Both knew it was a simple, clean, efficient way to cut the cord before it strangled them.

Edna embraced Liz. "Sometimes," she said, "strong people clash, making decisions neither wants. Often they're too stubborn to back down. If you find that's the case, don't wait too long. I may be Joe's mother, but I think he's worth any risk."

Using the back of her hand, Liz wiped away the tears. "Edna, did anyone ever tell you you're one smart lady?"

"As a matter of fact, Joe just did. Amazing how much alike you two are, isn't it?"

Liz sniffed. "I guess Joe doesn't have the skin of a businessman after all."

"If marriage was based on skin, we'd all be onions."

"Who said that?" Liz asked, wiping her eyes again.

"I did."

"It's awful."

Edna smiled. "I know. Now get dressed. Joe's downstairs playing one of those mindless television games with Jason. If you're going to leave my house, I want to see you sweep down those stairs like the character you play on TV—completely sure of yourself."

Liz clung to her. Edna smelled of cinnamon and flour. "What are you baking?"

Edna's voice cracked. "Jason's favorite cookies. Fiona gave me the recipe."

"Why are you so good to me?" Liz asked.

"Because you're a nice person," Edna said simply. Her smile was warm. "You and Jason are always welcome."

Jason took his leave without realizing he really was leaving. He looked upon the ride as a jaunt, like one of many he'd taken with Joe and Liz. Wide-eyed, he bubbled with a million questions on the way to the little house Liz had rented the previous day.

Joe unloaded the suitcases. With each case he felt he was saying good-bye to the most important people in his life.

"What are we doing here?" Jason asked, seeing the small house and tiny enclosed yard. "Who lives here?"

"We do," Liz said. The house was in a residential neighborhood. There were tract houses next to the tiny plot of ground. The view couldn't hold a candle to the view from Joe's house.

Jason looked around. "All of us? It's too small for Grandma and Grandpa." His face lifted expectantly.

Joe hung back. This was one time Liz could break her son's heart without him being there to soften the blow. Instinctively her eyes lifted to his, pleading. Muttering a soft oath, he bent down until he was eye level with Jason. The boy flung his arms around Joe.

"Nothing's changing except your address, sport. We'll still see each other. Your mother thinks it best if you guys have a place of your own."

He scowled. "Why? For how long?"

Joe rubbed Jason's shoulder. "While you're in Colorado."

Liz picked up a suitcase. "Jason, you'll love it here. You've got a room of your own. Mike can come over to play with you."

His lower lip trembled. "Who's going to take care of me while you work?"

Liz lifted a lock of blond hair from his forehead, gently putting it back. "I thought I'd take you along. Will you like that?"

"I guess." He didn't sound enthusiastic.

Joe brought the rest of their things into the house. He slapped the key into her palm. The finality of what was taking place filled him with rage. Impossible woman!

"I'll see you later, Liz. Fran offered to drive the car over that you've been using."

"Joe," Liz said quietly. "I've rented a car."

His blue eyes smoldered. "Suit yourself. You always did do things your way." He left. For the first time he didn't kiss Liz good-bye, only Jason.

Jason clumped through the house, his crutches creating a hollow sound on the bare floors. He was back quickly. Liz began the task of unpacking and found Jason in the bedroom doorway, his bottom lip curled in disgust.

"I don't like it here," he declared, his whole manner accusing her of betrayal. "I want to live with Joe."

Liz sucked in her breath. It was the first time Jason had ever called Joe by his name. Wasn't this what she'd wanted? She'd been so worried about Jason's happiness, worried that if he called Joe Daddy it might hurt him. "Honey, we have our own house now, like we do at home."

"You promised," he accused, his sullen face condemning her.

"Let's call Fiona and find out about Herman and Ferdie."

"You call." He stomped out of the room.

"Wonderful," Liz sniffed. Joe! she wanted to scream. Make this come out right. Sniffling, she knew he couldn't. It was up to her.

"Jason," she called. He banged his bedroom door shut. Now I've got both of them angry at me, she thought.

By the end of the week she was mad at herself too. The only time she left the house was to tape the show.

Edna visited, bringing a jar of preserves. "Plum jelly. Jason's favorite." Jason gave her a big hug and a kiss. He hid the jar of preserves in his room.

"In case . . ."

"In case what?" Liz asked, knowing Jason meant in case Joe came to visit. Plum preserves were Joe's favorite too.

Vernon stopped by on his way to the store. "How about my taking this little fella off your hands today, Liz?"

Jason couldn't wait to go.

Tom drove by Saturday morning. It was a conspiracy, she just knew it. "Saturday's my day off," he said, grinning the same wide, impish smile that first endeared Joe to her. "Joe and I are taking the kids on up to Pikes Peak. We're going to have a picnic too. This'll give the little wife a rest."

Liz didn't need a rest. She needed some fun. She'd planned to take Jason to the Garden of the Gods. It was a beautiful day. In fact, the color of the sky was the same shade as Joe's eyes.

Jason was in the car as quickly as his crutches allowed.

All of her rigid requirements hadn't gotten her anywhere. She saw Joe every day at the taping, but he was cool to her. She was miserable.

"We had a wonderful time, Mommy," Jason said upon his return, his cheeks red from the outdoors. "Joe's taking me fishing tomorrow."

She cried herself to sleep.

Shirley and entourage were hounding her daily for news of the wedding. Joe had said he'd take care of it. What was he waiting for?

"You're an actress," he'd told her, a cold chill in his voice. "Just go on pretending, Liz."

Fran phoned.

"Fran, I haven't seen my son more than a few minutes out of every day for the past three days. The family's swallowed him up. Last night he slept over your house, tonight he's sleeping at Edna and Vernon's. He insists he wants to be with Joe."

Frances said blithely, "I'm coming over, Liz. Don't knock it. Freedom is wonderful."

Freedom, not loneliness, Liz thought.

She'd been lonely before, but never like this. Never with this raw, wrenching aloneness tearing her apart. She lay in bed at night, endlessly considering the course she'd taken, the consequences of her actions, cursing herself for throwing away her chance. As if that weren't torture enough, Jason gave her the emotional cold shoulder, blaming her for taking him away from Joe.

Fran arrived within the hour. Liz poured iced tea while her guest took a quick tour of the two-bedroom cottage.

"Do you like living in this box?" Frances asked, returning to the compact kitchen.

Liz pretended to love it. Her bedroom was cramped, the bathroom fixtures needed new washers, the toilet burped when flushed. There hadn't been many homes to choose from that were furnished where the owners were willing to rent by the month.

"It's exactly what we need. This way there's less to clean."

Frances harrumphed, quirking her brow.

"I wasn't looking for something pretentious," Liz said.

"If I were an ad agency the only way I'd sell this place is by calling it cozy."

"So it's awful," Liz shrugged, glad to be free to tell the truth. "I've lived in worse."

Frances asked. "Liz, you're the only woman I've ever met who deliberately aims backward instead of forward. You had everything going for you." Frances became very interested in a butterfly design on the sleeve of her T-shirt. "Do you still feel the same way you did about his work?"

"Sure I do," Liz admitted truthfully. "But the thing I can't stand more is the idea that Joe isn't a part of my life."

She looked as miserable as she felt. Now that she'd started, Liz wanted to get it all out. "My son barely talks to me. Whenever we go to the studio he makes a beeline for Joe, then ignores me as if I'm a pariah. Tonight we're supposed to attend a stupid party Shirley's giving. Joe claims we have to go. It's a professional obligation. I get a headache just thinking about it."

Liz tucked a leg underneath her. "Joe treats me civilly in front of Jason, but he's created a wall around himself. I can't blame him. In the past week I've done a lot of soul-searching. The stand I took on his work pales in the face of the alternative."

Frances finished her tea. "Did I ever tell you about the time Tom proposed and I said no?"

Liz looked at her suspiciously. "Do you have stories you trot out to everyone, depending on the occasion, or just to me?"

Frances laughed. "Seriously."

Liz scoffed. "You told me you and Tom fell in love and got married."

They went outside into the backyard, and sat on the redwood benches. "That's not exactly the way it happened," Fran said. "Tom issued an ultimatum. You know how big he is; when he wants to be he can be very intimidating. He told me he loved me, loved Janice, wanted to adopt her. He also told me he refused to settle for an affair. It was marriage or nothing. For a man who had had his share of women, you can imagine how he shocked me. I learned later how I had hurt Tom. He thought I didn't trust him with my daughter's upbringing. Can you imagine?"

"Oh lord, what have I done?" Liz said.

"Nothing that can't be rectified, if you move quickly. Don't forget, Shirley's about to announce to her readers that you and Joe are getting married."

Liz chewed the inside of her cheek. For the first time that afternoon, she brightened. "Do me a favor, Fran. Invite Jason to spend the night at your house."

A big smile creased Fran's face. "Oh, and what are you going to do?"

Liz punched her arm. "Play the most important role of my life."

Francis hugged her. "Shirley will be delighted."

"Shirley be damned. This is Joe, Jason, and my future I'm thinking of."

After Fran left, Liz phoned Joe. At first the line was busy. She kept dialing for half an hour. The minute she heard his voice she plunged ahead.

"Joe, what time are you picking me up tonight?"

She kept her voice carefully modulated, lest he suspect anything different in her attitude. She planned on wearing her blue sequin gown, dressing as if she were giving a live performance in front of a packed theater. She knew from experience that this particular dress evoked memories. The last time she wore it, they'd spent the evening making love. Later he told her never to throw the dress away.

"We'll have it enshrined," he'd said.

Joe told her he'd pick her up at five-thirty. When he hung up he was scowling. "It's now or never, buddy." He dialed a number. When he'd completed his call a slow grin spread over his face. He had another call to make. This call was a little more difficult, but Shirley understood.

The final call was to his brother. "The heck with what she thinks she wants," he told Tom. "I took matters into my own hands. Liz is the most stubborn woman I know."

"A perfect match," Tom said. "Are you sure this plan of yours is going to work?"

He passed a hand over his chin, recalling the chain of events. "It has to. I've tried everything else. All I can say is she'd better be pleased I'm planning on producing another radio show."

Joe arrived on time, complete with a wrist corsage of orchids. The jewelry box in his pocket was for later. If he had to ram the ring on her finger, so be it. As he told Tom, "A man's gotta do what he's gotta do." Liz could throw out her chin all she wanted. He'd take immense pleasure in realigning her scrumptious body.

A nervous Liz ushered him him. "You look wonderful, Joe. I've never seen you more handsome."

Those were his lines. "You look good too—beautiful, in fact." He'd never seen her so glamorous, so gorgeous, so delicious-looking. She must have worn her blue sequin on purpose, knowing how he loved it. Her hose twinkled a silvery sheen, and she wore high heels.

"I'm glad you approve," she said. "Care for a drink?" Before he could answer, he watched her swing her little hips from side to side. She poured two flutes of champagne, handed him one, and they clinked glasses. "A votre santé."

"We're late," Joe stated. He had the key to the honeymoon suite at the Broadmoor in his pocket.

Liz had never felt so fragile, so in need to be touched and held. Joe and Jason were her life, her reason for being, the precious people from whom she drew her strength.

She straightened up, lifting her eyes so Joe could see and hear her message. "Joe, I've got a proposition for you."

He didn't want to hear it. He was certain she was about to say he should get another co-anchor, that they'd made a mistake.

"Can't it wait until later?" He tapped the face of his watch.

"I don't think so."

"All right." He'd hear her out, then drag her through the door.

"What have you told Shirley, Joe?"

Joe studied her face before answering. "Nothing yet."

She breathed a sigh of relief. "Then may I?"

"Fine. Let's go," Joe said.

"No!" Liz said more sharply than she intended.

"I think I'd like to run through my lines first, the way we do at work."

"Go ahead," he said brusquely.

Liz stepped closer. Her eyes glittered, their shine reflected in his. Their clothing made the initial contact. She lifted a hand to his cheek, giving him a whiff of her perfume.

"I thought I'd start by letting Shirley—she did say her column ran in five hundred newspapers, plus all that other stuff she brags about?"

Joe nodded. "Something like that." He fingered the box in his pocket. As long as this was Liz's last hurrah, he could be generous about her kidnapping, postpone it a few minutes. Later she could rant and rave all she wanted. She'd have to do it as Mrs. Joseph Michaels, wife of a producer of radio shows, actor if he chose.

He'd had a week to think it over. Liz was going to marry him. No ifs and buts. If he had to go out of town, he'd take Liz and Jason with him. If it interfered with Jason's schooling, they'd hire a tutor. The important thing was not to let Liz get away.

Liz smiled warmly. "My lines might not be right, but here goes." Her gaze sizzled as she brought her shoulders back, lifting her chin. Joe sat down and spread out his legs. "You're on."

"Shirley, thanks but no thanks. We don't want your frills and hoop-de-la. Our wedding is going to be private. The only thing I want our public to know is that I love Joe with all my heart."

Liz held her breath.

He closed his legs. "Marriage, huh?"

She bobbed her head.

"Suppose," Joe countered, with an easy arrogance that made her squirm, "suppose good old Shirl wants to know where we're going to live?"

Liz sat down. She touched him. She hadn't planned to. It was reflexive, more to give herself courage. With one finger she traced his lips, lingering near a corner of his mouth. Defensively, her arms went around his neck. She wasn't going to let him get away this time.

"Joe, aren't you going to help me?"

"Uh-uh," he said, his heart swelling with joy. But the contact was too much for both of them—having been denied pleasure, they now eagerly sought it. Liz kissed the lips she'd come to know, the only ones which could ever claim her heart again.

His eyes shone into hers. "You were saying," he reminded her finally.

"Shirl, it's none of your business. However, in our family we go where the work is. Whenever possible, we'll adjust out schedules."

"But what about Jason? He's bound to have to change schools."

"Shirl, where've you been? This is a mobile world we life in. Jason will thrive. He'll meet new friends, become more self-assured. The only constant he needs is our love. Joe and I have enough love to go to the moon and back. Jason will be protected by that, even if we have to be apart some of the time."

"In other words, quality time?" Joe said, grinning, knowing how she hated that phrase.

She glared at him before kissing him. "Shut up, Shirl," she growled.

"And what if Shirley asks how you feel about a husband who travels? If he has to, that is."

"I'll learn to live with it." It was the best she could do.

Joe pushed her away. "Sorry, it won't work."

Liz was beside herself. What had gone wrong? She'd planned this seduction scene to a T. It had worked when they'd done a similar one on *Happy Town*. She'd thrown herself at him again, only to be rejected.

"Dammit, not again." She stalked away from him. "Why not?"

"You botched it up." He tapped the toes of his shoes together.

"Botched what up?" She couldn't breathe.

He flicked a spot of lint from the couch. "I wanted to kidnap you. You took all the fun out of this."

"Are you crazy?" she screamed, stamping her foot. "I just told you I loved you. I want to marry you. I'm willing to go out and buy a matched set of luggage. I threw myself at you and all you can say is some nonsense—"

He was grinning broadly.

"Wait a minute! Why did you want to kidnap me?" She was grinning now too, closing the space between them.

He grabbed a handful of hair. "I had this idea that after the party I'd lock you in the honeymoon suite until you said yes."

"Oh yeah? How would you have made me say yes?"

He whispered in her ear.

She loved everything he suggested.

"Do you want to hear what I'm going to tell Shirley?" he said. Liz nodded.

"Shirley, I'll say. We're going to live right here in Colorado when we're not in New York. There's going to be none of this separation business. Liz will continue her career as long as she wants, or until the first baby comes. Then we may have to reopen negotiations. In the meantime . . ." He dug into his pocket. "This is where I hand her my new business card."

Liz's heart soared as she read the imprint. "This is really yours?"

"There were other styles, but Jason chose this. My folks like it too." Liz squealed.

"Your mother said you belonged in business." She kissed every spot of exposed flesh her lips could find. "Joe, did I ever tell you how much I love you?"

He slung her over his shoulder, carrying her into the bedroom. "What are you doing? We have to go to the party," she protested. "My dress. My hair."

"Damn, you're noisy." He slid her down in front of him. "Anyway, we don't have to leave."

She began to wiggle out of the dress. "You said five-thirty."

He grinned. "But I didn't say what for. I took the liberty of telling Shirley something pressing had come up. I canceled."

She giggled. "You mean we've got the whole night to ourselves?"

"Uh-huh. This is stage one. Think of this as one of those progressive dinners. Later we'll go to the honeymoon suite."

"What honeymoon suite?"

He took a long time kissing her breast. "The one I booked."

She gasped. "I already said yes."

"Spoilsport. I still want to kidnap you."

"Just a minute."

"What?"

"I can't go to a honeymoon suite with messy hair. You're going to mess my hair."

"Count on it," he said, his throat thick with emotion. He followed her down, removing the blue velvet box from his pocket. He rested it between the valley of her breasts. "In case you're shy," he teased, slipping the marquise-cut diamond onto her finger. "I don't want you completely naked."

She clasped him to her, whispering against his mouth. "Silly man. That's exactly the way I want you."

"By the way, we're having two best men," he said.

"Who?"

"Tom and Jason."

Somehow that didn't surprise her.

THE EDITOR'S CORNER

This summer Bantam has not only provided you with a mouth-watering lineup of LOVESWEPTs, but with some excellent women's fiction as well. We wanted to alert you to several terrific books which are available right now from your bookseller.

A few years ago we published a unique, sophisticated love story in the LOVESWEPT line called **AZURE DAYS, QUICKSILVER NIGHTS** by talented author Carole Nelson Douglas. Carole has an incredible imagination, and her idea for her next project just knocked our socks off. Set in Las Vegas, **CRYSTAL DAYS**—a June release—and **CRYSTAL NIGHTS**—a July release—are delightfully entertaining books. Each features two love stories and the crazy character Midnight Louie, who can't be described in mere words. Don't miss these two summer treats.

Speaking of treats, Nora Roberts's long-awaited next book, **PUBLIC SECRETS,** is on the stands! Nora's strengths as a writer couldn't be showcased better than in this riveting novel of romantic suspense. **PUBLIC SECRETS** is summer reading at its very best!

Now, on to the LOVESWEPTs we have in store for you!

Suzanne Forster writes with powerful style about characters who are larger than life. In **THE DEVIL AND MS. MOODY,** LOVESWEPT #414, you'll meet two such characters. Edwina Moody, hot on the trail of a missing heir to a fortune, finds her destiny in the arms of an irresistible rebel named Diablo. Edwina is more than out of her element among a bunch of rough-and-tumble bikers, yet Diablo makes her feel as if she's finally found home. On his own mission, Diablo sees a chance to further both their causes, and he convinces Edwina to make a bargain with the devil himself. You'll soon discover—along with Edwina—that Diablo is somewhat a sheep in wolf's clothing, as he surrenders his heart to the woman who longs to possess him. Much of the impact of this wonderful love story is conveyed through Suzanne's writing. I guarantee you'll want to savor every word!

This month several of our characters find themselves in some pretty desperate situations. In **RELENTLESS,** LOVESWEPT #415 by Patt Bucheister, heroine Dionne Hart takes over the helm of a great business empire—and comes face-to-face once again with the man she'd loved fifteen years

(continued)

before. Nick Lyon remembers the blushing teenager with the stormy eyes, and is captivated by the elegant woman she's become. He's relentless in his pursuit of Dionne, but she can't bring herself to share her secrets with a man she had loved but never trusted, a writer who couldn't do his job and respect her privacy too. But Nick won't take no for an answer and continues to knock down the walls of her resistance until all she can do is give in to her desire. Patt will have you rooting loudly for these two people and for their happiness. If only men like Nick could be cloned!

Talk about a desperate situation! Terry Lawrence certainly puts Cally Baldwin in one in **WANTED: THE PERFECT MAN**, LOVESWEPT #416. What would you do if you'd just dumped the latest in a long line of losers and had made a vow to swear off men—then met a man your heart told you was definitely *the one!* Cally does the logical thing, she decides to be "just friends" with Steve Rousseau. But Cally isn't fooling anyone with her ploy—and Steve knows her sizzling good-night kisses are his proof. He takes his time in wooing her, cultivating her trust and faith in him. Much to his dismay, however, he realizes Cally has more than just a few broken relationships in her past to overcome before he can make her believe in forever. And just when she thinks she's lost him, Cally learns Steve really is her perfect man. All you readers who've yet to find someone who fits your personal wanted poster's description will take heart after reading this lively romance. And those of you who have the perfect man will probably think of a few more qualities to add to his list.

If you've been following the exploits of the group of college friends Tami Hoag introduced in her *Rainbow Chasers* series, you're no doubt awaiting Jayne Jordan's love story. in **REILLY'S RETURN**, LOVESWEPT #417, Jayne finds the answer her heart and soul have been seeking. Since Jayne is quite a special lady, no ordinary man could dream of winning her. It takes the likes of Pat Reilly, the Australian movie star the press has dubbed the Hunk from Down Under, to disturb Jayne's inner peace. As much as she'd like to deny it, all the signs point to the fact that Reilly is her destiny—but that doesn't make the journey into forever with him any less tempestuous. Tami has an innate ability to mix humor with tender sensuality, creating the kind of story you tell us you love so much—one that can make you laugh and

(continued)

make you cry. Don't pass up the opportunity to experience a truly memorable love story in **REILLY'S RETURN**.

At last Joan Elliott Pickart has answered your requests and written Dr. Preston Harper's story! Joan has received more mail about Preston Harper over the years than about any other character, so she wanted to take extra care to give him a special lady love and story all his own. With **PRESTON HARPER, M.D.**, LOVESWEPT #418, Joan fulfills every expectation. As a pediatrician, Preston's love for children is his life's calling, but he longs to be a real dad. The problem is, he doesn't see himself in the role of husband! When Dinah Bradshaw walks into his office with the child who's made her an instant mom, Preston's well-ordered plans suddenly fall flat. But Dinah doesn't want marriage any more than Preston had—she's got a law career to get off the ground. Can you guess what happens to these two careful people when love works its magic on them?

Next in her *SwanSea Place* series is Fayrene Preston's **THE PROMISE**, LOVESWEPT #419. In this powerful story of an impossible love Fayrene keeps you on the edge of your seat, breathless with anticipation as Conall Deverell honors a family promise to Sharon Graham—a promise to make her pregnant! Sharon vows she wants nothing else from the formidable man who'd broken her heart ten years before by claiming that the child she'd carried wasn't his. But neither can control the passion that flares between them as Sharon accepts Conall's challenge to make him want her, make his blood boil. You've come to expect the ultimate in a romance from Fayrene, and she doesn't disappoint with **THE PROMISE**!

Best wishes from the entire LOVESWEPT staff,
Sincerely,

Susann Brailey

Susann Brailey
Editor
LOVESWEPT
Bantam Books
666 Fifth Avenue
New York, NY 10103

FAN OF THE MONTH

Mary Gregg

Reading has always been a part of my life. I come from a long line of readers who consider books treasured friends. I cannot imagine a life without books—how dull and bland it would be.

LOVESWEPTs are *the best* contemporary romances due to one lady, Carolyn Nichols. From the beginning Carolyn promised quality not quantity, and she has kept her promise over the years.

Some of my favorite authors are: Sandra Brown—she must use her husband as a hero model; Kay Hooper, who I can always depend on for her wonderful sense of humor; Iris Johansen; Helen Mittermeyer; Linda Cajio; Billie Green; Joan Elliott Pickart; and Fayrene Preston, who reminds me a little of Shirley Temple.

At the end of the day I can curl up with a LOVESWEPT and transport myself back to the days of my childhood, when Prince Charming and Cinderella were my friends. After all, romance stories are modern fairy tales for grown-ups, in which the characters live happily ever after.

60 Minutes to a Better, More Beautiful You!

Now it's easier than ever to awaken your sensuality, stay slim forever—even make yourself irresistible. With Bantam's bestselling subliminal audio tapes, you're only 60 minutes away from a better, more beautiful you!

__ 45004-2	**Slim Forever**	$8.95
__ 45112-X	**Awaken Your Sensuality**	$7.95
__ 45035-2	**Stop Smoking Forever**	$8.95
__ 45130-8	**Develop Your Intuition**	$7.95
__ 45022-0	**Positively Change Your Life** ...	$8.95
__ 45154-5	**Get What You Want**	$7.95
__ 45041-7	**Stress Free Forever**	$8.95
__ 45106-5	**Get a Good Night's Sleep**	$7.95
__ 45094-8	**Improve Your Concentration** .	$7.95
__ 45172-3	**Develop A Perfect Memory**	$8.95

- -

Bantam Books, Dept. LT, 414 East Golf Road, Des Plaines, IL 60016

Please send me the items I have checked above. I am enclosing $_____ (please add $2.00 to cover postage and handling). Send check or money order, no cash or C.O.D.s please. (Tape offer good in USA only.)

Mr/Ms _____

Address _____

City/State _____ Zip _____

LT-5/90

Please allow four to six weeks for delivery.
Prices and availability subject to change without notice.

THE DELANEY DYNASTY

THE SHAMROCK TRINITY

THE DELANEYS OF KILLAROO

THE DELANEYS: *The Untamed Years*

THE DELANEYS II